Riders

Heck Carson Series: Volume 1

John Spiars

Riders of the Lone Star   John Spiars

Version 1.0 –October, 2017

Published by Under the Lone Star Books at CreateSpace

ISBN: 978-1978276369

Discover other titles by John Spiars and read his monthly blog at underthelonestar.com

TABLE OF CONTENTS

CHAPTER ONE

1852

It promised to be a typically hot and humid South Texas day, as Jesse "Heck" Carson swung into the saddle and prepared to leave his home. The sun was just beginning to crest over the hills that bordered his family's ranch, and the morning haze bathed the pasture in a purplish hue that seemed to capture the somber mood of the occasion.

Heck turned to take one last look at the adobe ranch house where he was born, and assuming it might be for the last time, he lingered over the scene for just a moment. He then lightly touched the appaloosa's side with his spur, urging her down the dirt path.

"C'mon Cheyenne," Heck said softly. "We gotta make at least thirty miles today."

Heck had spent all of his sixteen years on the ranch, and he was trading the safety of her comfortable confines for an unknown future. The smell of honeysuckle hung thick in the morning air, and their vines obscured the split-rail fence that surrounded the house. He led his appaloosa through the narrow gate, and then climbed down to close it. He could have done this from the saddle, but he wanted to take his time and have one last look around before leaving for good. It was sixty-five miles to San Antonio and he hoped to make half that distance before dark, so he spurred the appaloosa to a trot and never turned back.

He looked out over the gently rolling hills and deep valleys populated with cottonwood, cypress, and mesquite trees. The call of a few birds was the only sound breaking the stillness of the early morning quiet. Heck followed the Pedernales River trail for a few miles until it crossed the main road leading from Fredericksburg to San Antonio.

The South Texas "Hill Country" always held wonder and mystery for Heck, but now, traveling alone, he was nervously scouring every ridge line, hoping not to see the ominous silhouette of Indians on horseback. For more than a few hapless settlers, that had been the last sight they would ever see. The men and women were usually killed and scalped, but the children were generally taken by the tribe and either kept or sold to another tribe as a slave.

Even nearby Fort Martin Scott was not much of a deterrent. There were only a few hundred cavalry soldiers stationed there to cover hundreds of square miles. Soldiers from the fort and Texas Rangers from San Antonio would often stop by the Carson ranch to rest and water their horses, and Heck would take the opportunity to listen to their stories.

It was the Texas Rangers that he liked most of all. He was drawn to their reputation for fierce determination and unflagging bravery. Stories of great Indian battles and wild chases on horseback filled his daydreams. He could imagine himself pursuing some desperate foe, while bullets and arrows whizzed over his head.

Heck wanted to live these adventures, instead of just dreaming about them. He was determined to explore the world and see all of the things he had only read about in books, and he had no desire to spend his days chained to the same piece of ground year after year.

He left this last part out when he told his father he was leaving, but it didn't seem to make much of a difference. His father had barely spoken to him in the years since his mother died, and after he decided to leave, the man didn't speak to him at all. His brother, Jefferson, seemed almost relieved that Heck was leaving, as he had grown tired of having to play peace maker between his father and brother.

The sky was aflame in shades of orange and brown as the sun dipped beyond the western horizon, and Heck stopped to make camp for the night. Heck stared down into the shallow valley, however, he wasn't really looking at the scenery, but what lay beyond. At this moment, as the stars were just beginning to illuminate the dusk sky, Heck knew he was making the right decision. Thoughts of home and family slipped from his consciousness, and were replaced by images of daring pursuits, nights spent under the stars, and the excitement of facing down dangerous outlaws. He would ride between the Red River and the Rio Grande, bringing law and order to those that wanted to peacefully settle the frontier, and his bravery would be a thing of

Ranger legend for future generations. He spread out his bedroll a few yards off the trail, and these thoughts fueled his dreams as he quickly drifted into a peaceful slumber.

CHAPTER TWO

For a sixteen-year-old who had never been more than a hundred miles from the place of his birth, San Antonio was the center of the world. As the second largest city in Texas, it had everything: hotels, saloons, and the Mercado, where with enough money, a person could buy goods from all over the world.

As he rode down dusty Main Street, Heck took in all the sights and sounds of the city. Everywhere was a flurry of activity. The market was bustling with people selling their wares. The stockyards exploded with commotion; cowboys whooping and hollering while bringing in their cattle. A lively tune flowed from the keys of a piano being played in one of the many saloons. Heck recognized the tune, but couldn't think of the name.

He turned his head from side to side as he slowly rode along the crowded street, not wanting to miss any of the sights. Most impressive of all was the Alamo, the shrine to over three-hundred brave men who were more like gods than just heroes to Heck. Men like Davey Crockett, Jim Bowie, and William Travis were everything that Heck grew up believing real men should be. They were remembered as he himself wanted to be remembered, as heroes who gave everything they had for a cause they believed in. The sight of that stone structure was what really convinced him that he had made the right decision in leaving home.

Making his way past the clapboard store fronts, livery stables, and cattle pens, Heck finally saw the sign that he was looking for, "Office of Texas Rangers Company C." It was an unassuming wood framed structure at the end of Main Street, next to a shop that advertised Painless Dentistry. Heck had never been to a dentist, but he figured if there was such a thing as painless dentistry, they wouldn't need to put it on the sign.

Climbing down from the weary appaloosa, Heck paced up and down in front of the office for ten minutes, trying to muster up the courage to go in. He couldn't help being worried. What if they didn't want him? Where would he go? He couldn't go back home that was for sure. Finally, he made up his mind and turned the brass knob of the old wood door and stepped inside.

The Ranger office was small. It was comprised of a small outer office, a room off to the right containing a bed and night stand, and in back was a wooden door with bars across the top that probably served as the jail cell.

In the outer office, behind a small wooden desk, sat a man of no more than forty with a weathered face half hidden by a large handlebar mustache. His hair was salt and pepper colored, but neatly combed and he wore a white shirt with a fancy red vest. Pinned to the vest was a Mexican peso, which served as the Ranger badge.

"Are you Capn' Hale, sir?" Heck asked, with as much courage as he could muster.

A pair of haggard blue eyes peered over a steaming coffee cup, undoubtedly trying to size up the boy that was interrupting his morning routine.

"It's just Captain Hale. What do ya need boy?" came the gruff response.

Heck tried to decide whether he should answer or just run out as fast as he could and get back on his horse.

The man behind the desk set his coffee cup down and with a look of impatience mixed with mild amusement, asked again, "What do ya need boy?"

Heck knew it was now or never, so he blurted out the whole speech he had rehearsed just as fast as he could. "My name is Jesse Carson, but everyone just calls me Heck and I came here cause I want to join up and be a Ranger."

The Ranger captain shifted his gaze from Heck back to his coffee cup, "I don't have time for no nonsense, boy," He said.

Heck took a step backwards toward the door and grabbed the door knob, ready to get out of there, but suddenly remembering that he had nowhere to go, he stopped and steeled himself to his mission.

"It's not nonsense sir. I want to join up and be a Ranger." Remembering the rest of his speech he continued, "I can ride and shoot better than most and I ain't afraid of nothin'."

With the last part of his speech, he knew he was skirting the truth a bit. It was true enough, he could ride and shoot, but he had no idea whether he was better than others or not. As far as not being afraid, well that was just a flat lie. In fact, he was more nervous right now than he ever remembered being. He felt he was not making much of an impression on the captain, and needed to come up with something fast. While he hadn't received the response he had hoped for, at least he hadn't been thrown out of the office either.

All of a sudden, the Captain broke into a booming laugh and slammed his hand on the desk. "Yes, I can tell that you're not boy. Now where are your parents?" he said, ready to get back to work after this amusing distraction.

Heck thought for a moment how best to answer the Ranger's question, and feeling that the truth was always the best policy, answered him, "I've left home sir. Left to be a Ranger. I told my Paw what I wanted to do and he said fine. So, I left."

"Well your Maw will be missing you," Captain Hale said. "Now like I said, you better just get on home."

Heck dropped his head and started to head out the door, when he came up with one last idea. He decided to just tell Captain Hale everything.

"My Maw's dead, sir. She's dead and my Paw don't care what I do. So, I want to be a Ranger. I got nowhere else to go, sir."

Heck spoke these words while looking Captain Hale directly in the eye; a quality that Hale always considered an excellent sign of character.

Standing up, the Captain walked around the desk to where Heck stood. The Ranger Captain towered over the teenager, who was almost six foot tall himself. Sizing the boy up again, he asked, "You say you're not afraid of anything. Is that right?"

"Yes sir!" Heck said.

With a serious expression, the Captain asked, "Are you crazy or just plain dumb?"

Confused, Heck could only manage to reply timidly, "Sir?"

Hale looked down at the boy and said, "Well, someone that's never afraid is either crazy or dumber than a hay bale. All I want to know is which one are you?"

Collecting himself and beginning to feel more than a little insulted, Heck shot back, "I ain't crazy or dumb, Sir. I just want to be a Ranger."

Captain Hale walked back to his chair and a big smile came over his face. "It's okay, boy. The Rangers put a lot more stock in bravery than smarts anyway." His laugh put Heck at ease and made him nervous all at the same time. "I reckon you got gumption enough for five men," Captain Hale continued, "What's your name, boy?"

Heck drew a quick breath, the first he'd taken since walking into the office. "My name's Jesse Carson, Sir, but most people just call me Heck."

The Ranger pulled on the ends of his mustache with the tips of his fingers. A look of puzzled interest showed just below the surface of his rock-hard features. "Why would anyone call you that?" the Captain asked, no longer with just feigned interest, but with genuine curiosity.

"I don't know, sir. That's just what everyone has called me since before I could remember," Heck said, feeling a little embarrassed. If people called you Heck, then it makes since that you should know why.

Captain Hale let him off the hook by changing the subject. "That's fine, Mr. Carson. Now ya say ya know horses, do you?"

"Yes sir, I sure do," Heck said, a broad smile coming across his face. "I was raised on a ranch and I've been around horses my whole life, Sir."

Captain Hale nodded his head, "Well, that's fine boy, but if we're going to get along, you need to stop calling me Sir. You will address me as Captain Hale or just simply Captain. I've earned the rank, but Sir makes me sound like I don't work for a living." Deciding to have a little more fun, he yelled, "Is that what you think boy, that I don't work for a living?"

Caught off guard, he shook his head and stammered, "Well, no sir, I uh, I mean no Captain."

"Glad to hear it," Hale said. "Now, I need someone to help with the horses; mainly to feed and water them, clean stalls, and brush them down. You think you can handle that?"

Without waiting a second, Heck blurted out, "Yes, Cap'n, I can surely handle that."

Trying to determine if he was making the right call, the Ranger looked at the youngster and then extended his hand across the desk, "Ok, then you're hired. The job only pays four dollars a month plus room and board, but there's no room in the bunkhouse right now, so you'll have to sleep in the livery stable. There's a loft with a bed, but that's about all I can offer you right now. Can you live with that?"

Still shaking the Captain's hand, Heck readily agreed.

Taking his hand back, Captain Hale pointed the way to the livery. "You'll be working for Old Tom. He's a fair man, but he does not suffer shirkers, so do what he tells ya."

"Yes sir, Cap'n," Heck said, backing out the door.

"It's Captain," Hale said. "I've earned the whole rank and I'd be obliged if you would use it." "Yes Captain," Heck said.

CHAPTER THREE

Walking into the livery, Heck saw a tall, lean figure brushing down a horse with a curry while humming a sad tune. The man's features were obscured by a long gray beard. His head was covered with a worn-out hat; the brim of which was pulled down low almost completely concealing the old man's eyes. His skin was weathered and tanned, undoubtedly from many years in the sun. His clothes were old, but clean, and his boots showed equal age, but were of the highest quality. He had the look of someone accustomed to life outdoors with few comforts.

"Are you Tom?" Heck said, hating to interrupt the tune.

The older man spoke without stopping his work. "I am, and who are you, young man?"

15

Heck liked him right away and quickly answered, "I'm Jess, but most people just call me Heck. I just joined the Rangers and Cap'n Hale told me to find you. He said I would be working for you."

Old Tom ran his fingers through his long gray beard as if trying to dislodge some unseen object, but as Heck could tell, he was actually sizing up the young man to see how much trouble the Captain was throwing him.

After a brief moment, he decided that perhaps the kid might be useful and stuck out his long bony hand, "Good to have you aboard. I guess if the Captain says you're okay, I can find something for you to do around here. Do you know anything about horses?"

"Yes sir, I sure do," Heck said proudly. "I've been around horses all my life."

Tom smiled and tossed Heck the curry, "That don't mean doodly. I've been around women my whole life and I sure as hell ain't got them figured out. Let's see what you can do with that curry."

To Tom's surprise, the boy really did seem to know a lot about horses, and more importantly, he was someone who hadn't heard any of his stories and would not roll his eyes every time he started to relate some past experience.

Over the next several weeks as Tom instructed him on his new duties, Heck learned the man's life story, and what a life it was. Old Tom had been born and raised in Kentucky on a small farm in the great mountains along the border with Virginia. After leaving home, he made a living in the mountains as a trapper, trading with both Indians and Whites alike, but it was the Indians that fascinated him the most. He came to adopt many aspects of their culture and even lived with the Shawnee for a short while.

16

Seeking adventure and possibly to escape some entanglement with the wife of a Shawnee brave, Tom followed others from Kentucky to Texas. He had fought under General Sam Houston for Texas independence. With the establishment of the new Republic of Texas, law and order was needed, and Tom joined the newly formed Texas Rangers. With his extensive knowledge of Indians and survival in the wild, he thrived in his new job.

In his almost twenty years with the Rangers, he had fought Cherokee, Apache, horse thieves, murderers, and Mexican outlaws. After the Mexican War, he decided he was tired of fighting and only agreed to stay with the Rangers in a limited, behind the scenes way. He now ran the livery, keeping the Rangers' horses, and acting as an elder statesman and advisor to the younger men. He took great pride in the fact that there was not a better looking or more well maintained herd of horses for five-hundred miles.

Heck not only learned many things about training and caring for horses, but also what it meant to be a Texas Ranger. He was taught the pride and sense of responsibility one should have every time they put on the Ranger badge. Heck was instructed in the history and traditions of the Rangers. He learned the names and stories of the famous Rangers who came before; men like John Coffee "Jack" Hays and Bigfoot Wallace. These men were held up as what every Ranger should aspire to be, and Heck came to idolize each and every one of them. Meer admiration wasn't enough, Heck wanted to surpass them all and be the best Ranger ever.

Old Tom was not his only mentor. Heck learned everything he could from each Ranger in Company C; Rangers like Jim King.

Jim King was an expert gun hand who had joined the Rangers five years earlier with his brother Henry. He was a small man in his early twenties, with a jovial manner that belied his ability to kill when the situation called for it. This combination of wit and a fast gun was very attractive to the ladies, and he certainly returned their affections. He wore his pistol in a cross-draw holster for quick access, but also because he liked the way it looked.

Jim agreed to help teach Heck to shoot and the art of the quick draw, but he made him promise to never use it unless he had to. Heck saved his money and purchased a Walker Colt from Old Tom. The gun was old, but in good condition and it shot straight. Every day after he had finished his work, he would go down by the river and practice drawing and firing at old bottles. After a few weeks, he had developed calluses on his thumb from pulling back the hammer so many times, but he was quickly becoming an excellent pistolier. When the bottles became too easy to hit, he started shooting at old playing cards, and then would tear them in half to make even smaller targets.

"You keep that up and you'll be the best shot in Texas," Jim said one day after watching him shoot. "Just remember that being able to hit paper targets is one thing, but being fast and accurate in a fight is something else altogether. Playing cards don't shoot back, and I've seen plenty of good target shooters freeze in battle and get themselves killed."

That's one thing that Heck had been able to figure out on his own. "How will I know if I'll be good enough in a real fight?"

Jim put his hand on the boy's shoulder and said, "Well boy, unfortunately that's something you'll have to learn from experience. You'll either have what it takes, or you won't. It's not the fastest draw or even the best shot that wins the day. Nine times out of ten, it's the man that keeps his head and doesn't panic who comes out alive. That's the best advise you'll ever get from me."

Heck didn't know it then, but he would eventually get more experience than he ever wanted.

Heck knew that there was a lot more to being a Ranger than just being good with a gun. He learned how to track from William "Bill" McGregor. He learned how to live off the land from Ranger Adolf Heilman, who was a German and the descendent of a Hessian soldier. As a young boy, he had lived with the Apache for seven years and from them he learned to survive in the wilderness with nothing more than his instincts and a sharp stick.

Henry King, Jim's older brother, was a champion pugilist who instructed Heck on how to fight with his hands. It was a useful skill, but one that came at a price. Henry believed the best way to learn how to fight was through experience, and as such, he never pulled a punch when training Heck. After several black eyes and one broken nose, Heck learned the art of ducking and dodging Henry's punches, while managing occasionally to land one or two of his own.

John Hagen was the Company's rifleman and he tried to make a marksman out of the young man, but while he became a fair shot with a rifle, both men knew that Heck would never be an expert.

The rest of Company C, men like Charles Wainwright and Bob Curtis, imparted their knowledge as well. Heck did his best to learn from each of them and repaid their efforts by making sure their horses were always taken care of and their equipment was always in tip top shape.

CHAPTER FOUR

"Stay on her boy. You got her now," Tom yelled from his perch on the top rail of the corral.

Heck was too busy trying to stay in the saddle to hear Tom's words of encouragement. Every time the grey mare would drop her head and kick her hind legs, Heck was sure he would come flying out of the saddle. He kept his seat and hung on to the rope more out of fear than from any kind of skill. When he had told the other Rangers that he had broke horses before, what he really meant was that he had seen his father and brother brake horses. As he was finding out, watching was a far cry from actually doing.

"You've got her right where you want her!" Tom yelled, as proud as if the boy was his own son. "Now ride her out. There you go." The Arabian mare finally stopped bucking and managed a fairly mild trot around the corral. Heck knew enough to quit while he was ahead, so he dismounted and handed her off to Old Tom.

Relieved that he was still alive and able to walk, he took a long drink from his canteen and gave a big boyish grin to Tom, who returned it with a hearty slap on the back.

"That's a good day's work son," Old Tom said. "I'm sure glad I've got you around to do the hard stuff, cause I'm getting too damned old to be breaking horses. When I saw you that first day you came to us, I never thought you would last. I thought for sure you'd light out as fast as you could within a week, and the Captain didn't think you'd last that long." Tom smiled giving him another slap on the back. "But you sure proved both of us wrong. I reckon we'll make a Ranger outta you yet. Let's you and me go see what Ms. Mulita fixed us for dinner."

Mulita cooked for the company, and Tom always said her tortillas were worth crawling across a briar patch for. She had long black hair which she usually wore pulled back on top of her head and held in place with a colorful scarf. The Rangers all talked about how pretty she was, and while Heck agreed that her tortillas were wonderful, he chose to defer to the others regarding her appearance, as they had more experience with the fairer sex.

She cooked in the café during the day and made extra money in the evenings mending the Rangers' clothes. She was polite, but kept her distance from most of the men of Company C. However, she always went out of her way to be nice to Heck. Mulita always fussed over him, making sure that he ate enough and that he had clean clothes. She was the only one he had ever known, besides his mother, who had worried about such things. He didn't understand why, but he felt comforted that she was around and worried about him. Mulita had no family, but all the Rangers commented that she would have no trouble finding a husband if she ever wanted one.

Over the next two years, Heck worked with the company horses and learned everything that he could get Old Tom and the rest of the Rangers to teach him, and he learned well. Old Tom had commented on more than one occasion that there wasn't a man in the Company who knew more about horses than Heck; himself included.

Heck continued to practice with his pistol every day, and before long, he could draw and shoot the center out of the ace of spades at twenty feet. When he felt he was good enough with his right hand, he started practicing with his left. He practiced so often, he had to start making his own shot because he went through so much ammo that he could no longer afford to purchase it. Heck felt this would be a useful skill to have, and as time would tell, he was right.

While he was happy in his duties, he longed for the opportunity to become a real sworn Ranger. Despite all of his improvement, Captain Hale still hadn't let Heck go out on patrol yet, so he was still untested in the eyes of the Captain and the rest of the company. Heck knew from experience that pestering the Captain was not the way to go about getting what he wanted. Captain Hale was not a man to be persuaded by words, he had to see things for himself, and for now, he had not seen anything that convinced him Heck was ready to ride with the other men.

Chapter Five

1854

Walking down the street to the Ranger's barracks, Heck was intent on finding some way to show the Captain that he was ready; that he could pull his own weight with the other men on patrol. He was lost in thought, with his head down, as young men are want to do when working through some weighty problem. Not watching where he was going, he walked right into another man walking the opposite way down the wooden boardwalk.

"What the hell are you doing, boy?" The other man snapped, obviously drunk.

"Sorry, sir," Heck stammered. "I didn't see you."

The drunk grabbed Heck by the front of his shirt. "You need to watch where you're going, you stupid kid. If you're too dumb to walk the street with men, then you need to stay at home with your mamma."

The man continued to hold on to Heck's shirt and push him down the street. Heck looked around and saw that everyone on the street had stopped and were looking at them, curious to see what would happen next. Old men sitting along the boardwalk had stopped in mid conversation, shop keepers were standing with their brooms, and men walking down both sides of the street turned and watched the altercation. Worst of all, there were women. Heck could see ladies, arms full of their recent purchases, watching to see what this drunk man was going to do with the boy. Most were hoping not to see any bloodshed, while others, whether they wanted to admit it or not, hoped that they would. With intent interest, everyone watched this scene play out in front of their eyes.

Heck knew he had to do something, but all he could manage was a feeble, "You better let me go, mister."

The drunk man just laughed, "What are ya going to do if I don't, boy? Huh? Just what the hell are ya going to do?" The drunk stopped pushing and pulled Heck's face within an inch of his own. They were so close that Heck could smell the stale whiskey on his breath, mixed with the sweat from his unwashed clothes. Heck knew this man was just drunk and mean enough to not care what happened next. He wanted a fight and Heck had given him all the excuse he needed. Heck tried to talk his way out of the situation.

"Look, mister," he said, "I don't want any trouble. I'm sorry I ran into ya and I promise not to let it happen again."

The other man was not going to let him off that easy though. He sized Heck up and then said, "I'll tell ya what, boy, you get on your knees and beg me not to give you a beating and we'll call it square. Otherwise, I'm going to beat you within an inch of your life in front of all these people."

Heck looked around at everyone gathered and then back at the drunk. He was the same height as Heck, but outweighed him by at least fifty pounds. His arms were as big as both of Heck's combined. He had probably been in dozens of fights before, both drunk and sober, and he could undoubtedly handle himself. If Heck fought him, he knew he would lose. The only question was how bad the drunk man would beat him, so Heck did the only thing he could think of. Looking down, he raised his foot and with the heel of his boot stomped on the other man's foot as hard as he could. The drunk instantly let go of Heck's shirt and limped backward crying out in pain. Heck remembered thinking that he should take the chance to run off, but there was no way he was going to let some drunk get away with embarrassing him in front of half the town.

Remembering what Henry had taught him, he made a fist and as soon as the other man turned to face him, Heck aimed a punch right at the bridge of his nose. Heck heard the crack of the man's nose as he made contact. As the drunk stumbled backward again, Heck stepped in with another punch aimed at his temple, but the more experienced fighter caught his fist in his hand and flung him to the side. Heck lost his balance and stumble to the right. Trying not to fall to the ground, Heck did not see the punch coming, and as it made contact with his jaw, he was knocked off his feet. The pain in his jaw was immediate and intense, and it hurt worse than anything that he could remember. He tried desperately to get to his feet, but every time he put his arm down to raise himself up, the drunk man would kick him in the gut causing him to slump back down again. Lying on the ground, Heck tried to gasp for air, but the flurry of kicks had broken a rib and knocked the wind out of him.

"How do ya like that, boy? Huh? I bet you wish you had begged me now, don't you?" the drunk said while delivering more kicks to Heck's midsection and face. "Why don't you beg me now and maybe I won't kill ya?" The drunk was laughing, enjoying the beating he was delivering to this stupid kid. He was having so much fun, he didn't notice the man coming up behind him. "What's the mat—"

The drunk was spun around midsentence and came face to face with Henry King, who delivered a blow to the drunk man's nose. Henry was stronger and three inches taller than him, and his punch knocked the drunk off his feet. Reaching out, Henry grabbed the man by his long, stringy hair and jerked him to his feet. He delivered a quick jab to the drunk man's stomach, then another, and then one more before letting the man go. As he let go, the drunk hit the ground landing on his knees, at which point he received a boot heel to the teeth, knocking him on his back and relieving him of two more teeth. Standing over the beaten man, Henry asked through clenched teeth, "Have you had enough?" The man held up his hand to signal he wanted no more. Henry smiled, "I need to hear you ask me nicely to stop or I'm going to beat you from one end of town to the other." The drunk raised up, and with blood dripping from his broken nose and busted mouth, he politely asked the Ranger to stop.

Bob and Adolf grabbed the drunk and dragged him off to jail, while Jim and Captain Hale carried Heck to the Doc's office. The brief excitement was over, and everyone returned to what they were doing before. No one was disappointed in the outcome.

Heck spent the next two weeks laid up in bed with two broken ribs. The Doc looked in on him often, but other than bandaging the injured area, there wasn't much that he could do. The other Rangers came by when they could to try and raise Heck's spirits, keeping him up to date on their daily activities.

Mulita didn't leave his side for the first three days, doing her best to keep his fever down with cold cloths she placed on his forehead. She sang to him in Spanish, and told him about the small village in Mexico where she was born.

He finally started getting stronger day by day, to the point he felt he was ready to resume some of his normal duties.

"Are you sure you're ready?" Mulita asked, not convinced that Heck was strong enough yet.

"Thank you, ma'am, but I fell a lot better. Besides, the Captain don't tolerate no shirkers, and Old Tom needs my help with the horses and other chores."

Mulita smiled that sweet, comforting smile that Heck had come to enjoy over the last couple of weeks. In many ways, she reminded him of his mother, though she was much younger. She had the same ability to make him feel better just by being around. He had forgotten how nice it was to have a feminine presence in his life to balance the harshness of the daily routine.

"Don't try to do too much," she said. "You don't want to reinjure yourself. The world won't come to an end if the others have to care for their own horses for a while longer."

"I will be ok," Heck said. "Thank you for all of your help."

Smiling, Mulita turned and left him. She could not understand why anyone would choose the life of a Ranger as it seemed to her a lonely existence full of danger and ultimately death.

CHAPTER SIX

"I tell ya boys, we almost had that damn Indian this time. If we'd been able to find water, we would've had their heads on a pole by now," Jim said, driving the point of his knife into the table.

"Almost don't count for nothin' when it comes to Indians, Jim," Henry said. "It's bodies, and I didn't see ya bring any back; dead or alive."

John Hagen looked up from his breakfast, "I'll tell you one thing Henry, I had that damn Shaking Hand in my sights. If we had been able to get just a little closer, he would've been dead already."

Over a breakfast of tortillas and beans, the Rangers were indulging in their favorite pastime; bragging about their adventures and occasionally stretching the bounds of truth a bit just to make the stories a bit more entertaining.

Henry, having finished his breakfast, leaned back in his chair, "Let me ask you something, John. If you got that close, why didn't you just keep after them?"

John slammed his coffee cup on the table, "Henry, I just told ya we were out of water, and the Llano is a mighty poor place to meet your maker."

Henry knew as well as anyone that when it came to chasing the Indians across open country, the white man was at a serious disadvantage. The Indian was adept at riding long distances without water. They trained themselves to ignore hardships that would cause even the most ardent Indian fighter to head back to town. They could go for days without water, a week without food, and could ride without stopping. The Comanche were known for being able to sleep in the saddle, enabling them to keep moving for days at a time. They would ride until their horse dropped from exhaustion and then continue on foot until they could find another horse, and then start all over again.

The Comanche were a dangerous enemy and the Nokoni band were the most dangerous of all. Their leader, Shaking Hand, was a cunning, vicious foe, who had a hatred for whites. His bands of braves were known all across Texas, and they had a fearsome reputation. The Nokoni would raid a farm or ranch, kill all the adults, and steal anything of value; especially children.

"What makes you so sure it was Shaking Hand leading 'em?" Henry said. "He never comes to Texas anymore. He just sends his braves down here to do the stealing and stays up in Indian Territory in a nice warm teepee wrapped up with one of his wives."

John knew that Henry was right, but he was trying to do his part to liven up their adventure. "I had him in my sights. I know it was him, and I'll kill him yet."

Jim looked up from his plate, still clutching his knife and waving it in a sweeping gesture and said, "If anyone is going to kill that miserable thief, it's going to be me, and I'll kill a great many of his murdering braves right along with him."

Old Tom stood up and angrily said, "We ain't killers, Jim. We're the law, and as such, we'll bring those Indians in alive, if possible. It's up to the army to kill 'em if that's what needs to be done. You remember that, Jim. It's them that are the murderers, not us. They're the savages. I'll hear no more talk of killing at this table today. Come on Heck, let's get their horses rubbed down." Old Tom walked out of the Ranger's barracks followed reluctantly by Heck.

Heck hated leaving just when the stories were getting good. Listening to the Rangers talk about their exploits was almost as good as being there himself, and it made him feel like a part of the company.

While brushing the horses, Heck pondered what had been said in the barracks earlier. He had never heard Jim so angry before, or talk about killing, even though Heck knew that he had killed plenty. He had heard stories of some of the men that Jim had personally sent to hell. He had a reputation as a fast gun who would kill if he had to, but he much preferred not to use his gun if he could avoid it. While teaching Heck, Jim would always remind him that killing was a last resort only and should be avoided at all cost. Now he was talking about setting out to kill Shaking Hand and all his braves.

"Hey Tom," Heck said, "why does Jim want to kill the Nokoni? He always told me to never set out to kill a man, yet he wants these Indians dead."

Tom walked over and started applying liniment to the horse's leg. "About seven years ago, we came across a small ranch house in the Palo Duro Canyon, or actually what was left of the house. It had been set on fire and was still smoldering when we came across it. There were dead animals scattered all around the house; horses, cows, and several dogs. Inside the house were the bodies of a man and a woman. They were shot full of arrows, their throats cut and they were scalped. Their names were Frieson, and they had three children; Martha twelve, Louise one, and a son named Clinton. He was ten, I think. Like I said, the house was still smoldering, so we knew the Indians couldn't be far, and we took off after 'em. We'd been riding for two days when we came across the body of a small child. She had been slammed against a tree so hard it bashed her brains in. She was dead when we found her, but I don't imagine she died right away. I guess the Indians figured they could travel faster without her slowing them down. We eventually had to turn back for lack of water. We heard later it was the Nokoni and their War Chief Shaking Hand, who had raided the Frieson's ranch." Tom moved to the horse's hind legs, checking for any sores that needed treating. "Eventually, Martha Frieson was found," he said. "She had been traded to the Apache, and by then she had three children. She had no home to go back to, so she wanted to stay with the Apache, but the army wouldn't have it. They made her come back to Texas. I don't know what happened to her, but she would always be an outcast among White people. It'd have been better if they had left her with the Indians. At least she would've had some chance at a life." Finishing with the horse, Tom stood and stared off into the distance at nothing in particular. After a deep breath, he said, "Clinton Frieson was never found. The Rangers and the army looked for a while, but there had been so many other children taken since then that we had to concentrate on the ones whose trail hadn't gone cold." Old Tom made a cigarette, and savored the first long draw. "We had seen killings like that many times before. We'd seen much worse, so I don't know why that one stuck in Jim's crawl. I guess when you see enough meanness, it eventually just gets to you, but that's why Jim hates the Nokoni so much. I think he really will kill them if he ever gets the chance, and no matter what I said, I can't really blame him."

CHAPTER SEVEN

Freidrick Granger and his siblings were enjoying an all too infrequent day off from chores. It was a hot August day with little breeze. The oppressive humidity sapped the energy out of every living thing, except apparently the five Granger children. They had left the house before sunrise to pick strawberries along the creek about two miles from their home.

Having filled two tote sacks with the fat, candy red berries, they spent the rest of the morning playing tag under the old cypress trees that populated the fertile earth along the creek.

The five Granger children were: Freidrick age twelve, Eva ten, Carl nine, Johannes six, and Rebecca three. It was one in the afternoon when they started the long trek home with the treasure that their mother would soon make into mouthwatering pies and jars of sweet strawberry preserves.

It was a hard walk across open ground in the blistering midday sun. Being the oldest, Freidrick and Eva each carried a bag, while the younger children dragged themselves slowly along, complaining loudly with each step. With their thoughts focused on the heat and strawberry pies, the group didn't notice a band of painted riders watching them from a distant hilltop.

"I'm tired. How much longer till we get home?" Johannes said, falling back several feet from the rest of the group.

"We should be crossing into the south pasture around the next bend, but your crying won't get us there any faster," Freidrick said with a deep sigh.

Coming to the barbed wire fence that separated the south pasture from the open prairie, Freidrick lifted the middle wire to let the other children pass underneath. In the distance, sitting atop a small rise, the Granger farmhouse could be seen. With their home in sight, the children picked up their pace with visions of strawberry pies having been replaced by ones of a cool drink from the well.

"I've gotta rest a minute," Carl said, stopping in his tracks. "I'm about to die of thirst. Why didn't we bring a canteen with us?"

"Because we didn't," Freidrick snapped back.

"I wanna stop too, Fwedrick," Rebecca cried.

"We're almost home. Just keep walking," Freidrick said, picking Rebecca up with his free hand.

Carl didn't move. His attention was focused on something in the distance. Following Carl's gaze, Freidrick saw the five riders approaching quickly from behind them.

All of the riders and their horses were covered in war paint and were decorated with feathers.

"Indians! Run!" Freidrick said, dropping the strawberries and grabbing Rebecca with both arms. Their house was less than half a mile away, but Freidrick knew they could never make it. He only hoped the Indians would be slowed down getting over the fence, but a quick glance over his shoulder revealed they had cleared that obstacle with no problem.

"Come on! Run faster!" He yelled, willing his siblings forward. "We're almost there! It's just up the hill now! Just keep running!" Hearing the thunder of horse hooves, he shifted Rebecca to his left arm and started pumping with his right, desperately forcing himself forward, through shortness of breath and aching legs.

Reaching the base of the hill, Freidrick turned to help his siblings up the dirt path, but all three were on the ground screaming, with the Indians on top of them. Fearing they were dead already, he covered Rebecca's eyes and started scrambling up the path to the house.

"Fwedrick, I'm scared! Don't let them get me!" Rebecca cried.

"Shh. It'll be ok. We're almost home," Freidrick said between breaths.

Making it to the top of the hill, he followed the path to the front of the house; fear and anger carrying him further than his own endurance would have ever been able to. Rounding the corner into the front yard, he was not prepared for the sight that awaited him.

Lying just off the front porch was the lifeless form of a man with the top of his scalp missing; his blood pooled around his head. It was the body of his father. Freidrick tried to run in the opposite direction, but a pair of strong hands grabbed him from behind and Rebecca was ripped from his arms.

"Leave her alone! She's just a baby!" He screamed.

Kicking loose, he charged at the Indian that grabbed Rebecca. Hitting the brave with everything he had, Freidrick wrestled his sister away from the Indian. He tried to run, but felt his legs give out from under him and he fell to his knees. His vision was blurry and he had an intense ringing in his ears. The Comanche warrior stood over him, ready to deliver another blow with the butt of his rifle should he try to get up.

"Fwedwick! Fwedwick! Help me!" Rebecca screamed as the painted Comanche carried her to his horse.

The big Indian lifted her onto his horse and climbed on behind her. When she felt him release his grip, she scrambled off the horse, but her feet had barely touched the ground when he grabbed her long blond hair and jerked her onto the horses back. With one hand around the screaming child's throat, the Indian choked her until her screams became muffled gasps for air. Rebecca flailed her arms and kicked her legs, trying desperately to get loose, unable to get a breath. Finally, the Indian loosened his grip and she started coughing, taking short sips of air in between.

Slowly Freidrick opened his eyes, fighting through the haze, able to see only blurry images of what was happening around him. The ringing in his ears had not stopped. If anything, it was worse than it was before. He could see the Indians talking, but could not hear the words coming out of their mouths; not that he would have understood them had he been able to hear. He could feel something warm on the back of his head and it felt as if it were running down his back, soaking his shirt.

Slowly, Freidrick made it to his feet, trying to fight through the dizziness that engulfed him. The ringing in his ears was starting to subside and he began to hear sounds, but he was not able to distinguish them. They were just a jumble of unrecognizable gibberish. He stumbled as he tried to make his way to Rebecca, but he was intercepted by one of the warriors and pulled over to a horse.

"Fwedwick, you're bweeding," she said, between hacking coughs.

Freidrick stared at her as he was led to the other horse. He could tell she was saying something, but could not make out what it was.

There were three Indians in the yard, their faces and torsos painted with red and yellow streaks. They had black feathers in their hair and on their arms. They wore buckskin breeches and moccasins on their feet. The horses were also painted with the same red and yellow streaks, and their manes were braided with multi-colored beads and adorned with black feathers. Both horses and men were thin, almost malnourished looking, and covered with dirt and sweat, as if they had been on the trail for many days.

Freidrick was lifted up by one of the braves and sat in front of him on the horse. From horseback, he was able to once again survey the scene. He saw the body of his father lying on the ground, his shirt and pants covered in blood. He quickly averted his eyes and saw two more Indians coming out of the house carrying blankets, pots and pans. The two Indians clumsily carried their prizes from the house, dropping several of the household items as they went.

The warriors yelled at each other in short fragmented sentences, but Freidrick was unable to understand what they were saying. He was only able to infer their intent through their gestures.

Thoughts were whirling through Freidrick's mind too fast to comprehend. "What do they want with us? Where is Mama? Where are my other brothers and sister? Is father dead? Of course, he's dead. No one could lose that much blood and still be alive. What do I need to do? How do I get us out of this alive? I need to say something to Rebecca, but what? I need to try and keep her calm, talk to her."

"Rebecca," he said, as calmly as he could. "Just do whatever they tell you. Ok? Do you hear me?"

"Y-y-yes," she sobbed. "I hear you. I'll do what they say, Fwedwick. I promise."

The two Indians from the house loaded up their plunder and jumped on their horses, leaving various items scattered across the yard. The Indians turned their horses and headed away from the house, single file, down the path toward the river.

Freidrick started to panic. He hadn't seen his mother or siblings. Were they all dead? Were he and Rebecca the only ones left?

"Wait!" Freidrick said. "Where is my mother and brothers and sister? Where are they?" He turned, screaming at the Comanche sitting behind him, "Where are they?" He repeated, the panic in his voice increasing. The Comanche laughed and said something to the rest of his band that of course made sense only to them.

Bowing his head, Freidrick said a silent prayer that his mother and siblings were ok, and that someone would rescue all of them before it was too late. Freidrick vowed to do whatever it took to keep his sister safe, and to do that, he knew he must remain calm and follow the Comanche's orders.

After traveling for the better part of five hours, Freidrick's group stopped in a clearing along the river bank. This part of the Llano River was about fifty yards across and the brown water churned against the smooth rocks that peppered the surface. The Comanche drank from the river, drinking enough to sustain themselves, but careful not to drink so much that they would get sick in the hot sun.

The captives were seated on the bank while the horses were watered, but no water was given to them. Freidrick had been parched before the capture, and his throat now felt dry and blistered. He thought about running down to the river and taking his chances with the Comanche, but then he thought about Rebecca and his promise to protect her. These thoughts were interrupted by the sound of riders approaching from the trees. Freidrick turned and saw five Comanche braves and Carl, Eva, and Johannes were with them.

Freidrick grinned at the sight of his siblings, as he was sure that they had been killed. For a few moments, he wasn't worried about what was going to happen. His brothers and sisters were alive and that's all that mattered. He tried not to think about the fact that their father was dead and more than likely so was their mother. The siblings hugged each other and the girls started to cry from joy. The boys would have too, but they refused to cry in front of their sisters.

One of the Comanche made the children sit down in a circle and he stood guard over them, while the others greeted each other in a most friendly manner.

While he couldn't understand a word of their language, Freidrick knew they were discussing the raid. There were smiles, back slaps, and much laughter.

After a few minutes, the Comanche walked down to the river, and began looking at something with much interest. One of the Indians said something to the one standing guard, and he then walked over, grabbed Rebecca, and dragged her down to the others by the river.

"Bring her back here!" Freidrick shouted. "Leave her alone! What are you doing?" He jumped up and ran down towards the river, but before he could reach her, one of the Comanche jumped up and aimed his rifle at Freidrick's head.

Freidrick could not see what was happening at the water, but suddenly Rebecca started screaming. It was a horrible, pitiable cry of terror that Freidrick would remember for the rest of his life. Forgetting the risk of being shot down, he ran down the bank towards his sister, screaming her name as he rushed to her aid. "Rebecca! Please don't hurt her! Just let her go, please!" He pleaded as he ran.

He almost made it to her before being tackled by the Indian with the rifle. He kicked and clawed the ground, trying to make it to his feet, but his strength was no match for the strong brave.

Freidrick could hear Rebecca's screams and the splashing of water. "Please just let her go! I'll make her mind! She won't be any trouble, just let her go!" He gave up trying to get to his feet. He knew his only hope was to try and beg for his sister's life, but after a few seconds her screams changed to a muffled choking sound. The horror of what was happening to his sister was obvious to him and he tried fighting his way off the ground once again. The Indian holding him down finally let him up, and he scrambled to his feet and ran with everything he had down to the river's edge.

It was too late. He hit his knees as he saw the body of his sister being carried away by the rushing water. Freidrick charged the Comanche closest to him, but was knocked to the ground. Looking up at him, he saw what had upset his sister and made her start to scream so horribly. One of the Comanche was carrying a lance and attached to it were the bloody scalps of his parents.

Chapter Eight

Heck walked along Main Street to Ranger headquarters, having been summoned by Captain Hale. Stepping inside the office, he could see the Captain in his usual seat behind his desk, but unexpectedly Old Tom was also there, too. He was leaning against the wall nursing a steaming cup of coffee, and looking worried; an expression Heck had never seen on the face of his mentor.

"Good morning, Mr. Carson. Please sit down," Captain Hale said, gesturing toward the chair in front of him.

Heck knew he was in trouble for sure. Quickly, he started to arrange in his mind what he would say in order to try and keep his job.

"I've got a proposition for you, Mr. Carson," the Captain said. "I have some friends in Austin and I believe I could secure you an apprenticeship with one of them. I believe you're smart enough. You could have a fine future in business or perhaps the law. I want you to think about this very carefully son. I would arrange for you to move to Austin where you could study and embark upon a fine career. Texas won't always be a lawless frontier and it's going to need smart, young people like yourself to help it grow and prosper."

Heck didn't hesitate an instant. Looking the Captain square in the eyes, he said, "Captain, I appreciate your trust in me, but I want to be a Ranger. That's all I've ever wanted to be. This country still needs men to clean it up and that's what I want to do." He also couldn't think of a more boring way to spend his life than behind a desk studying law books, but he decided to keep this thought to himself.

Captain Hale nodded, in that manner of reflection which Heck had come to recognize as grudging approval. "Are you sure, son? I won't make this offer again."

"I'm sure, Captain," Heck said.

"Alright, Mr. Carson, you're getting your wish," Captain Hale said, as he slid a Ranger's badge across the desk. "I think you're ready. The way you handled that drunk a few weeks ago showed me you've got what it takes."

Heck looked down at the badge, and a huge grin came across his face. "But Captain, that man whooped me good. I thought you'd think I was too weak."

Captain Hale looked at him and said, "You stood your ground. You kept your head and helped apprehend a menace to this town. I could not have been more proud.

You just keep that same determination and you'll make a fine lawman. I am sending you out with Rangers McGregor, Hagen, Wainright, and the King brothers. Another ranch has been raided along the Llano River and five children were taken. I want to try and get these Indians before they can make it back across the Red River. Grab you gear and horse and be ready to ride in an hour."

Sticking his hand out, the Ranger captain congratulated the young man and wished him good luck. He hoped the boy was as ready as he had intimated, but there was no way to know for sure; not until he had been tested in battle.

After Heck left the office, Captain Hale turned to Tom, "Well, I can see you're itching to tell me what you think, so let's have it," he said.

Old Tom remained silent for a few moments before replying, "You made the only decision you could, Captain. The boy has to be tested at some point and I reckon now's as good a time as any. He's learned everything we can teach him. Everything else can only be learned from experience. He'll be going out with good men who'll do everything they can to keep him safe. From the moment he first walked through that door, you knew as well as I did that this day was bound to come. He's got the want to. Now we have to find out if he's got the grit."

CHAPTER NINE

Tom walked into the livery where Heck was loading his gear onto his horse. Heck stopped what he was doing and looked up as Old Tom spoke.

"Now don't go out there and get yourself killed. I've just started getting used to having you around and it'd be a damn shame if you went out and got yourself scalped. I'd have to start doing all of the work around here again, and I'm getting a bit too old for that."

Heck could see that his friend was worried, which disappointed him. He thought the old Ranger would be happy that the Captain trusted him, and believed he was ready to be a Texas Ranger. "Don't you think I'm good enough, Tom?"

The old man put a hand on his young friend's shoulder, "I think you can ride and shoot as well as any man around here, but it takes more than that to do this job and survive. Remember son, the most valuable weapon you've got is right here," he said, pointing to his head. "There are a lot of things that you need to learn that can only be learned from experience, and the trick is living long enough to get that experience. I've taught you everything I know, but you've got to take my advice and use it," Tom said, placing a hand on Heck's shoulder. "The Comanche are a deadly foe, but they prefer to have the element of surprise. If you can take that away from them, at least you'll even up the odds a little. Remember, always pay attention to the signs and you'll know when an attack is coming. It may only give you a slight advantage, but that could be the difference between life and death. You'll be out there in rough country that can be as deadly as the Comanche, but it can also be your best friend. Before an attack the air will change, it will get unusually quiet, and watch the birds. If birds take flight sudden like, that's a sure sign that something is about to happen. If they see that they've lost the element of surprise, they might even give up the attack. One more thing, if it goes bad a quick death is better. You hear what I'm telling ya, boy? Don't let 'em take you alive. The Comanche and Apache like to torture their captives before killing them; especially Rangers. A few years ago, a couple of Rangers from Company B let themselves get captured. A week later, their bodies were found and they had been cut to pieces and set on fire. Now these were brave men, maybe too brave. Instead of remembering to use their heads, they thought they could fight their way through anything. There's no shame in getting out of a bad situation. Live to fight another day, that's my motto. Your friends, Jim and John, are good men, but they take too many chances. Be careful of Jim, especially. He's got vengeance on his mind, and a man out for revenge can lose sight of what is important. These men are more experienced than you and you can learn a lot from them, but in the end, you have to take care of yourself."

Unable to think of any other words of advice, Tom stuck his hand out, hoping the kid would be ok. "You take care out there."

Heck shook the old Ranger's hand and mounted his horse. "Take care of things around here while I'm gone," Heck said, giving the old man a half smile.

"Will do, boy," Old Tom said with a wave of his hand.

Heck appreciated the words of wisdom from his friend. A man would have to be a fool not to learn from the experience of someone like Old Tom. Riding out into the street, Heck stopped to enjoy the moment. He was finally going on an adventure of his own and he intended to enjoy it no matter what the dangers were.

CHAPTER TEN

The Rangers rode through the night, arriving at the Granger Ranch just after sunrise. They had met up with a local sheriff who guided them to the ranch which was situated on the banks of the Llano River.

Time was not on their side. If they were to have a chance of rescuing the children, they had to overtake the Indians before they reached the northern border and made it into Indian Territory.

"They were Comanche, alright," Bill said, handling one of the many arrows scattered about the yard. "They prefer using cottonwood for their arrows and limestone for the arrowheads. It looks like their tracks head down to the river."

The sheriff nodded in agreement. "We followed their tracks as far as we could, and saw they took the river to the northeast. We lost the trail after about ten miles and turned back. They had at least a day and a half head start, and we thought it best to turn back and get help."

Bill shook his head and said, "That means that they're almost four days ahead of us; almost halfway to the Red River. Our only hope is that the children will slow them down and make them have to stop more often, but I wouldn't count on it. The Comanche aren't known for coddling their own children much less captives. If the children start slowing them down, there's the chance that they will simply kill them along the trail."

None of the Rangers wanted to think about that possibility, no matter how valid it might be.

"We're not going to find them standing here," Henry said, knowing they had at least a week's ride ahead of them. "Bill, you lead the way and we'll follow along behind you."

"Will do," Bill said, looking off into the horizon. "It won't be very hard to follow. It looks like they scattered their plunder as they went. They must have been in a real hurry to get out of here to leave all this stuff behind. These are valuable items for the Comanche. From the tracks, it looks like they made away with several horses. That was probably the real reason they were here anyway."

Riding down the rocky, limestone bank, Bill got off his horse and knelt down by the water. "They entered the river here and probably stayed in the water for several miles, trying to hide their trail. John, you and Henry follow me on the right side and Jim, Charlie, and the kid can take the left. If anyone sees any sign on the bank just call out."

Every so often they would find some item in the water that gave them assurance that they were still on the trail. Heck had no experience tracking Indians, but it didn't seem right that their trail was that easy to follow. He didn't want to question Bill or the other Rangers, but the words of Old Tom kept ringing in his ear, "Trust your instincts kid. They are good men, but they take too many chances." Heck admired each one of these men and wanted their respect, but he would come to regret not taking the opportunity to speak up when he had it.

"Over here, boys," Bill called out. "They came out of the river here. Look at all the tracks."   Tracks in the mud were evident along the rocky bank, and an obvious trail had been cut through the mesquite brush at the top of the four-foot bank.

It was only about ten in the morning, but Heck was already exhausted and sore from over two days in the saddle. He wanted a break, but there was no way he was going to appear weak in front of his comrades. Luckily, Henry spoke up and suggested they stop for a few minutes and water their horses while they had the chance.

Climbing from the saddle, Heck could feel his knees buckle, and he thought he would fall to the ground. Growing up on a ranch, he was no stranger to long hours on horseback, but they had been riding day and night, and it had taken its toll on his body. After stretching for a moment, he was able to walk, and he led his horse to the water. While she drank, he filled his canteen, and enjoyed being able to stand and walk around.

Henry took the opportunity to check on his companion. "There's no telling when we will come across fresh water again so be sure and drink plenty and fill up both of your canteens. We won't be turning back, and you don't want to be out on the prairie without water. Are you doing, ok? We've rode pretty hard and I know if I'm feeling it."

Heck nodded his head, "I'm doing good. Don't worry about me none."

Henry admired the kid's spirit, but didn't believe him for a minute. He just hoped it wasn't a mistake bringing him out.

Walking over to Jim, Henry told him to keep an eye on the kid. "I want you to watch out for Heck. He talks tough, but he's still green and there's no telling how he will handle himself if things go bad."

Jim frowned. He liked the kid well enough, but didn't like the idea of being made responsible for anyone but himself. "Why do I have to babysit him? If he wasn't ready, the Captain shouldn't have sent him out here. I've got all I can handle just keeping myself alive and trying to get those kids back without having to watch over Heck too."

Henry looked his brother in the eye and said, "You were green once too. Remember? You had me to look out for you. That kid's only got us. Like it or not, I'm making you responsible for getting that kid back alive. Got it?"

Jim just nodded. He knew better than to argue with his brother when he felt that strongly about something. He also knew that he wasn't going to let those Indians make it across the border. If it came down to a choice between getting the Indians or looking after the kid, he knew what he was going to do. Heck would be on his own.

The Rangers rode hard for over a week and didn't seem any closer to overtaking them. They had ridden out of the "Hill Country" and passed into the harsh terrain of the plains, where water was scarce. If they were attacked, there would be no place to take cover. They would be sitting ducks out in the open. The tall prairie grasses were perfect for concealing an attack party, so the Rangers would have to keep a keen eye every minute.

Bill McGregor had been able to track the Comanche, but was not sure how far ahead they were, or even where they were headed. The Comanche seemed to be moving in a zigzag pattern. They would be heading northeast, then suddenly cut back in a southeasterly direction. Their tracks would then turn towards the northwest before returning to their original course. Bill had been tracking since he was a boy, and realized this could mean only one thing. The hunters were now the prey.

CHAPTER ELEVEN

The Rangers arrived at the Brazos River near Parker County, and although all wanted to continue, they were exhausted and needed to rest. The spot they chose to make their camp was on a tall bluff overlooking the river and afforded a good view of the surrounding area. Its proximity to the dense woods was not ideal from a defensive standpoint, but they figured their enemy were miles ahead. They would be able to take advantage of the wild game the woods would provide, and after a good night's sleep and a hot meal, they would be ready for the long push to the Red River. The men were mindful of the urgency of their mission, but also knew that without some rest, they would be spent before achieving their objective.

Heck climbed off his horse and stretched his legs and back. It felt good to be out of the saddle for longer than just a few minutes at a time.

After taking care of the horses, the men fed and watered themselves. The cool water of the Brazos was very refreshing and the rabbits they had shot for their dinner made the tastiest meal that Heck could remember.

All of the Rangers enjoyed the rest, except, that is, for Jim King. He hadn't wanted to stop in the first place, and was eager to get back on the trail. "Why can't we just keep riding?" Jim said. "I don't like this waiting around. We should keep on the trail while we've almost got 'em."

Henry understood what his brother was saying, but he also realized that they were all spent and needed some sleep. "We needed to rest, Jim," Henry said laying out his bed roll. "It won't do no one any good if we're dead on our feet when we meet up with them. We'll be on the trail early in the morning, and that will have to do."

Heck drew the first watch while the rest of the Rangers slept. Looking up at the clear sky alight with stars, Heck thought about his home and family. He hadn't really thought about them in a while, but now, with nothing but time to think, he couldn't help wondering how his father and brother were doing. Heck wasn't homesick. Far from it. He was having the time of his life, but he hoped his father and Jefferson were well, and hoped he would be able to see them again.

As he walked the perimeter around the camp, Heck tried to recall everything that Old Tom had taught him about signs and how to read the signals around him. He listened to the sound the wind made through the trees. He could hear the gentle, soothing sound of the river just a few yards away. The song of the cricket and the male cicadas provided a pleasant aspect to the otherwise gloomy darkness of the forest. Heck didn't mind the loneliness of standing watch. He liked being alone with his thoughts at night. It gave him time to look back on all that had transpired in the years since he left home. Heck was barely eighteen years old and was already living out his dream. He was doing what he wanted to do for the rest of his life. A hand on his shoulder interrupted these thoughts.

"Get some sleep, kid. I'll take over from here," Henry said.

Heck smiled, and breathed a sigh of relief. "Thanks, Henry. I'm ready for a few winks."

CHAPTER TWELVE

"When is Bill going to get back?" Jim asked impatiently. The sun had yet to crest over the horizon and Jim had already saddled and loaded his horse. "I'm ready to get out of here. We're burning daylight, and you can bet them Comanche ain't sitting around no campfire sipping coffee. They're probably almost to the border by now."

Henry slapped his brother on the back and poured the last of the coffee. "We'll be heading out as soon as Bill gets back. It won't do us no good to ride out without a good idea as to where we're going."

Henry understood his brother's frustration. They all felt it, but out here, being impatient could get you killed. They all knew that it was better to let Bill scout out the area and get a clear idea of where they were going.

"I guess a good night's sleep and a hot meal just don't agree with you, Jim," Henry said, trying to lighten the mood and take Jim's mind off of the waiting.

"I'll enjoy both back in San Antonio," Jim said, in no mood to joke or have his mood lightened.

"I'd just as soon finish this job as quick as we can and get back there too," John said, "but I'll wager it's not the hot meal he wants to get back to. It's Mulita."

John Hagen never missed an opportunity to needle Jim. "We've all seen you sneaking over to her place of an evening, and I bet it ain't for a second helping of her biscuits neither."

This observation evoked much laughter from everyone, except Jim and Heck. Since he was new to the group, Heck didn't feel comfortable joining in on the ribbing. Heck decided it best to stay out of it, so he went down to the river to water his horse one more time before they headed out.

"Now see what you've done, John," Henry said. "You made the kid leave, and you know he's sweet on Miss Cortez too. I believe him and Jim will have to shoot it out to decide who will win her affections." He shot a smile at Jim and all the men burst out laughing again.

Disgusted, Jim swallowed the last of his coffee. "You need to shut your mouth, Henry. I've had about enough of your jokes."

Like most brothers, the Kings had a way of getting under each other's skin, and Henry was a master at it. Even as kids, it only took a little needling by Henry and they would end up fighting. Their mother would have to get in between them to make them stop. Both men were now standing nose to nose, neither willing to back down and diffuse the situation.

"You'd better take about two steps back, Jim, before I whip you like when we was kids," Henry said.

Jim stood his ground, staring his brother in the eye, not wanting to lose face in front of the other men. Henry tried once more to end it before it led to a fight that neither one wanted.

"I can still whip you Jim and you know it. You might be better with a gun, but unless you plan on shooting me, you need to get out of my face," he said, giving his brother a slight shove and bringing his hands up to a fighting stance.

Jim put his hands down and walked away. "We don't have time for this now, but we'll finish it back in San Antone."

Charlie turned from the entertaining scene playing out before him toward a sound some distance away. "Hey, what was that?" Charlie asked, straining to hear. "You boys hear that? It sounded like it came from the tree line."

"I don't hear nothing," John said looking around. "What are you spooked about Charlie, there ain't nothing—"

John Hagen stopped mid-sentence, as he tried to make out a figure emerging from the trees. The Rangers all drew their pistols, ready to fight, but were not clear what the situation was yet.

The figure stumbled out into the clearing, but in the half light of the morning the group could not make out who it was. With guns ready, all four men moved forward, trying to identify who the man was.

Jim was the first to identify the wounded figure. "My God, it's Bill," he shouted, running to the tracker's side. The big tracker was holding onto a tree to balance himself. After letting go, he fell face first to the ground.

Reaching his friend, Jim could see several arrows had pierced his back. He gently turned him over. "Bill. Bill. What the hell happened?" He asked, trying to determine the extent of his injuries.

Bill was conscious, but unable to speak. The other Rangers gathered around their friend, none sure what to do or say.

"Can you hear me?" Henry asked, scanning the tree line for any sign of the enemy. Charlie ran back to his horse to get his canteen, while Jim held onto Bill's head keeping him from rolling over onto the arrows sticking out of his back.

"Can you tell us what happened? Where are the Comanche?" Jim asked in a loud tone, hoping for some response.

Returning with his canteen, Charlie helped his friend sip the cool water, but Bill only choked and spit it back up. It was obvious to all that their friend and comrade would not make it. He had only minutes to live; five maybe ten, but no more. Bill was now coughing up blood.

"One of those arrows must have hit something inside," Henry said. "I'm afraid there's not much we can do for him."

John turned to Henry, "Let's get him on a horse and try to get him to a doctor."

Henry shook his head, "He'd never make it. He's too far gone. Besides, those Comanche can't be far behind. They'll be on us before we could get a mile."

Heck had finished watering his horse and was leading him up the embankment when he heard the commotion. Arriving at the top of the bluff, he saw a flock of birds take flight from the trees, and Old Tom's words sounded in his ear. "Watch for the signs, boy." He reached for his pistol, and had just pulled the hammer back when the first war whoops were heard. They were followed by a volley of arrows and the sound of a large group coming through the forest.

Like a west Texas thunderstorm, arrows rained down on the Rangers in torrents. Jim used his body to cover Bill McGregor, but it was a useless gesture. The tracker had breathed his last.

The Comanche poured out of the trees and descended on the Rangers in a violent fury, firing arrows and bullets as they ran toward the small group.

Heck fired at the charging warriors from the edge of the bluff, trying to remember everything that Jim had told him. "Remember to breath. Squeeze the trigger, don't pull it. Aim for the center of the body. Above all, remain calm and keep your wits about you. The man who walks away from a gunfight is the one who keeps his head and doesn't panic. Being fast helps, but calm and collected wins the day."

Heck calmly crouched down, took aim, and fired the Walker Colt at the closest Indian. He saw his target drop and he picked out another, and then another. The big pistol was heavy in his hand and jerked each time he fired, but it also felt natural, like part of his hand. What did not seem so natural was killing the Comanche. Heck had only known them as friends and teachers, not enemies. He had never seen them in battle and was shocked at their ferocity but also at what a majestic figure these warriors effected. Their faces were painted in black and white, and they wore eagle and turkey feathers in their hair and on their bodies. Their weapons were ornamented with brass and silver tacks. Had they not been intent on killing him, he would have found the whole scene utterly breathtaking.

Lying on their stomachs, Jim, Charlie, Henry and John did their best to fend off the war party. It was the fiercest battle that any of the group could remember. They tried to make themselves as small of a target as possible by lying as flat to the ground as they could. Arrows were landing all around them, and bullets whizzed by their ears like gnats. Dirt was churned up all around them by the incoming fire.

All the Rangers continued firing, not sure how many of the enemy there were, but certain that they were woefully outnumbered. The smoke from the continuous gunfire had obliterated all sunlight and enveloped the whole scene in an ominous gray fog.

The battle was obstructed by the thick smoke, and Heck could hear yelling and pistol fire, but could see nothing. Unable to fire, he stayed crouched on the ground, waiting for the smoke to dissipate so that he could see the enemy.

Out of the smoky mist, two figures emerged dressed in buckskins with painted faces. They each carried a lance in one hand and a tomahawk in the other. Both Comanche were running straight at him, closing the distance between themselves and Heck at a tremendous speed.

Having no time to take careful aim, he raised the Walker and fired from pure instinct, but his shot missed its target. Cocking the pistol again he fired, and again the bullet sailed wide of its target. The two warriors were within eight feet of him and he knew his next shots would be his last.

"Remember kid, stay calm. The cool head walks away from the battle." Jim's words came back to him once again.

As fast as he could, he pulled the hammer back and fired. The first Comanche jerked once and hit the ground. The other warrior was no more than two feet away now. Heck wondered if he had another bullet left. Had he fired five or six shots? He couldn't remember. Saying a silent prayer, Heck pulled the hammer back and looked at his approaching enemy. The point of the warrior's lance was inches away from his chest when Heck pulled the trigger. The barrel of the Walker was almost touching the chest of the charging Indian. Heck heard no sound, but saw the smoke pour out of the barrel. The big warrior dropped to his knees, and fell on top of the young Ranger.

The weight of the large brave pinned Heck to the ground. He tried to rise, but could not. Struggling to get the heavy warrior off of him, Heck saw the figure of the other Comanche rise from the ground and stumble toward him. Blood poured from the wound in his stomach and it was obvious that he was in much pain, but he kept his feet and made his way toward Heck.

Even in the midst of fighting for his life, Heck could not help being impressed with the determination of his deadly foe. Unable to get to his feet, Heck cocked the Walker still in his right hand. He was not able to raise his arm and take aim, so he had to turn his hand at an awkward angle and just estimate his shot. The Indian, silhouetted in the half-light of the morning sun, stumbled ever closer, with a look of inhuman determination on his painted face. Heck had only seen that look in the eyes of animals; animals attacking their prey, and moving on pure instinct.

As the Comanche stood over him, Heck pulled the trigger, but only heard the sickening sound of metal on metal. The gun was empty. He let the pistol fall from his hand and looked up at the black and white painted face of the figure standing over him. With a fluid motion, the Indian rolled the lifeless body of his comrade off Heck, and then quickly grabbed Heck around the neck with one hand.

Heck had no sooner gotten the weight of one Indian off him than he had another holding him down. The Indian crouched on top of him, his knee pushing into his abdomen. It was all Heck could do to remain conscious, as his very life was being squeezed out of him. He tried, but could not muster up the strength to force the Indian off of him. If the warrior had been content in merely strangling the young Ranger to death, the Comanche might have lived to kill again, but he had no intention of letting his enemy off that easily. He wanted to inflict pain, and see that pain in the young man's eyes. The Indian held the Ranger by the throat with his left hand and with his right produced the biggest knife that Heck had ever seen.

Unable to move under the big Indian's weight, and feeling as if he would lose consciousness any minute, Heck franticly felt inside his boot for the stag handle of his own knife, hoping he could reach it before his enemy drove the blade of his weapon into his stomach.

The Comanche warrior had killed many times, but he wanted to savor this one and make it last as long as possible. He held the knife over his head, relishing the fear alive in Heck's eyes.

As the warrior brought his knife down towards its mark, the Indian felt a sharp, burning pain, like being dipped in boiling water. With that first thrust, the brave let go of Heck's throat. He cried out in pain, stunned by the unexpected attack.

Not content to merely wound his adversary, Heck pulled the knife from the Comanche's side and thrust the blade deep into his lower back. With the second thrust, he was able to roll the warrior off of him and get to his feet. Heck climbed on top of him and stabbed him in the heart, making sure that he was down for good this time.

Satisfied that his enemy was dead, Heck got to his feet, feeling neither guilt nor pleasure about what he had done. He just felt glad to be alive. Knife in hand, he spun around, expecting to face more attackers. As the smoke cleared, he saw no one; no Comanche or Rangers. Walking to where his comrades had been moments before, he saw the lifeless forms of several Indians and several friends.

The first one he recognized was Henry King. He had been shot with several arrows and his throat was slashed. The sight of his friend and fellow Ranger covered in blood almost made him puke, but he knew it would serve no purpose. He felt it would be an insult to the memory of such a fine man. The other Ranger was Bill McGregor, who had somehow made it back to the group. Heck was glad that at least he hadn't died alone.

The other Rangers were nowhere to be found, and he decided they must have pursued the Indians into the woods. Heck knew he had no choice but to go looking for them.

He searched until he found two pistols that were still loaded. One had three rounds left and the other two. With a pistol in each hand, Heck entered the woods, scanning both right and left as he moved from tree to tree as carefully as he could.

Walking as silently as he could, he calculated each step, careful not to step on any twigs or rustle any leaves. This was a skill, ironically, he had learned as a boy hunting with his Comanche friends along the Perdernales.

Heck came to the edge of a small ravine, maybe six feet deep. It had once been a creek, but was now strewn with dead and decaying trees. It was too long to go around, but would provide the perfect spot for an ambush if the Comanche were waiting for him. He had two choices, either risk a crossing or go back to the horses and wait for the rest of his party to return.

Heck decided to cross the ravine, but he would have to be especially careful, as the deadfall would pose considerable risk, and could easily give away his position. Starting down the steep slope, he held onto old roots sticking out of the ground, easing himself down at an angle, trying to make as little noise as possible. Halfway down, he grabbed onto a long root about three inches in diameter and used it as a rope to descend the remaining two or three feet.

At the bottom, he had to climb over and then under the decaying remains of an old oak, having to stop several times to untangle himself from the sharp briar that had grown in and around the old tree.

The air was completely still, with not a breath of wind, and Heck was sweating profusely. The lack of wind combined with the high Texas humidity created a stifling atmosphere. He stopped for a moment to wipe the sweat from his brow and caught a slight movement up ahead. He heard a brief rustling of leaves, but could not tell what it was or where it came from.

With both pistols drawn, he proceeded even more carefully; conscious of every step. After about ten feet, he stopped and listened, trying to make out any noise that didn't belong. He heard what at first he assumed to be the wind or the sound of running water. It was a soft, muffled sound; like escaping air. Cocking his pistols, Heck moved slowly toward the sound. As he scanned every direction, the beating of his own heart drowned everything else out. Climbing onto the rotten remnants of a cottonwood, he looked left, right, and directly ahead trying to find the source of the sound, but could see nothing.

Stepping down, his foot sunk into the leaves that covered the creek bed. The smell of decaying wood and vegetation saturated the area, causing the already stagnant air to become almost unbearable. Taking another step, Heck felt the grasp of five fingers around his ankle. He wheeled around, but could see no one.

Concealed beneath the rotting leaves, barely noticeable, was the almost lifeless body of Ranger Charlie Wainright. Heck knelt down and carefully dug away the leaves and uncovered his comrade. "Charlie, it's Heck. What happened to you?"

Ranger Wainright tried to speak, but he was unable to produce words. He gasped and attempted to cough, which caused blood bubbles to form at the corner of his mouth.

"It's okay, Charlie. Don't try to speak," Heck said. "Let me tend to your wound and then I'll
    work on getting you back to camp."

The leaves that had covered his body were soaked in blood, as was his shirt and face. It took only a moment for him to pinpoint the injury; a deep gash around his throat. It was a wound that even Heck knew to be fatal. Charlie had covered the wound with his hand, but this had done little to stop the flow of blood, and it was a miracle that he had not already bled to death.

Heck could do nothing for his friend, and he tried to think of something to say, but no words came to mind. He wanted to help his friend and comrade, but there was nothing to be done.

It took only a few minutes, and then Charlie Wainwright was dead. He didn't want to leave his friend there, but he knew he must find out if anyone was still alive. There was nothing to do, but keep going.

Knowing very well that the enemy could be waiting to slit his throat too, Heck proceeded slowly up the other side of the ravine, digging his fingers into the soft earth in order to pull himself up.

Reaching the top of the bank, Heck surveyed the area, trying to take in everything from the brush and thickets to the tops of the trees. It looked as if he were on the edge of the woods which opened into a clearing fifty yards ahead. The Indians, if still around, had concealed themselves very well.

Unable to detect anyone, he quietly got to his feet and started making his way to the clearing. He still used the trees as cover, carefully watching where he put each step.

Heck was very thirsty and his throat was parched and sore. He would have to get back to the river soon or risk heat stroke from lack of water. Hiding behind a large oak, Heck surveyed the whole clearing, and had made out the spot where the Indians had hobbled their horses. Heck figured they had made their way through the woods just as he had done, obviously knowing the area far better than he had. The Indians knew that it would make sense for the Rangers to stop for the night at the river and that it would be a perfect place for an attack. Heck's instincts were right, the Comanche had lured them into an ambush.

The sound of crunching leaves brought him back from his thoughts. Listening, he could tell that they were no more than a few feet behind him. He still held both pistols, but whoever it was had the drop on him.

Heck didn't like his odds, but he also didn't like the thought of being shot in the back or having his throat slit like Charlie. He let the pistol in his right hand drop to the ground and tried to keep the other one hidden. Slowly he turned around, positive that he would be shot.

"Kid? My God, it's good to see you!" John Hagen said.

Jim King was with him, and Heck was as relieved to see them as they were him.

"Dang kid, we thought for sure you were dead by now," Jim said shaking the young Ranger's hand.

Heck smiled, "It was pretty touch and go there for a while, but I'm still here."

"You sure are," John said. Then with a look of disappointment, he added, "The Comanche are gone. We just missed them by a few seconds."

Heck nodded, lowering his head. "Bill and Charlie are dead. So is Henry," he added, looking at Jim. "I'm real sorry, Jim."

"Thanks kid," he said, placing a hand on his back. "I knew he was killed, I just didn't want to believe it was true."

Looking up at the sky, John sighed, "Well, I guess we'd better get back. I want to get our fellas buried before the animals get to 'em." His eyes met Jim's and he said, "I'm sorry, Jim, I just meant that—"

"It's alright, John. You're right, we'd better get their graves dug."

CHAPTER THIRTEEN

By the time they had finished burying their dead it was late in the afternoon, and John was anxious to get on the trail back to San Antonio. "We need to get back and notify the army. Maybe they will be able to find the kids in Indian Territory before they get too far."

Jim shook his head, "We ain't going back to San Antone just yet. We can still catch 'em if we ride hard. Those kids are slowing them down. They have to rest and stop more often for water. That will give us the advantage."

"Are you crazy?" John shot back. "There are only the three of us against God knows how many of them. Don't tell me that you didn't notice that they were Nokoni Comanche."

Jim turned his back and continued packing his horse, "Yeah, I noticed they were Nokoni, but what difference does that make?"

"It makes a difference because you know as well as I do that this was a trap. It was a trap from the very beginning, and you don't care. You want vengeance so bad that you're willing to ride into a bad situation just to satisfy your need for revenge. We are only three men, and there is no way that we can win this. They've already killed Bill, Charlie, and Henry. Do want them to kill the rest of us, too?"

Jim turned and walked toward John, "It's real easy for you to just ride away. It wasn't your brother that they killed. It wasn't your kid that they stole, and it wasn't your family that they murdered. They've been raiding into our territory for years and we ain't done nothin' about it. Well I'm tired of just letting them go. I'm going to finish this once and for all, and you can ride back to town if you want to, but I'm going after them."

John understood Jim's feelings. He wanted to put these Indians in the ground too for what they had done, but he knew that getting themselves killed wasn't going to solve anything. "We're not going with you. Me and the kid are going back to San Antonio. On the way, we'll stop at Fort Gibson and let the army know what's happened, and if you're smart, you'll go with us."

Jim glared at John with a look of hate, mixed with utter disappointment. He was disappointed in his friend, but deep down he knew that John was right. He had no right to ask them to go along on what probably amounted to a suicide mission. Jim knew that the odds were against him, and that he would probably get killed, but he didn't care. He was going after the Nokoni, and he was mad that his friends weren't going with him. Lifting himself into the saddle, Jim turned his grey Arabian around and started after his prey. Thinking about it though, he wasn't sure who was the prey and who was the hunter.

On the ride to the fort, Heck had plenty of time to think about everything that had happened. He had been tested in battle and had come out alive, but three good men had not. They were men who were far more experienced in fighting Indians than he was. Heck had gotten the adventure he had hoped for, but he knew that there was a price to be paid and death was merely the final payment. This revelation, however, did not change his mind. In fact, he was more certain than ever that being a Ranger was what he was meant to do. These men were his brothers, and there was no way that he was going to let one of them ride off to their death alone. Heck reined his Appaloosa to a stop, "John, I'm going after Jim. I can't let him do this alone."

Stopping his horse, John grabbed Heck's arm and said, "Now listen to me kid. Those Comanche killed his brother, so I can understand how he feels, but the only thing that Jim's going to find is his own grave. He's a grown man, and can make his own choice, but there's no way I'm going to let you go and get yourself killed too. The only hope that he has is us getting word to the army as quickly as we can."

Heck knew that John was right, but he also knew that he could get word to the army alone. "You can do that by yourself. You don't need me, but Jim might. I'm going to ride back to him. I hope you reach the fort in time. Believe me, I don't want to die, but I'm not going to let Jim face them alone."

John could see there was no arguing with him. "Okay kid. I don't have time to argue with you, but I still think you're being foolish. I'll try to get help in time." Sticking his hand out, John said, "You did real good out there today. We weren't sure how you'd be in battle, but I was real proud of you. I hope I get the chance to buy you a drink when all of this is over."

Heck smiled, "I hope so, too. Good luck, John." Both men turned their horses and rode off in opposite directions.

Chapter Fourteen

The scorching noon sun was beating down and Jim kept his horse moving at a slow trot, so as not to overheat horse or rider. He was not very familiar with this area, and didn't want to miss any signs of his quarry. There would be a waxing moon tonight, which would hopefully provide enough light so he could keep riding. He had gotten through the more rugged part of the Brazos River Valley and hoped to be in the plains by sunset.

The heat of battle had passed and Jim had nothing but time to think about his plan. The thought that he could die out here left him more frightened than he wanted to admit. He had grown up with the same belief as most boys, that being brave meant having no fear of death, but he also knew that was just what boys told each other when they were dared to do something dumb. He had seen enough battle and death to know the difference between real bravery and cowardice. He only hoped that when his time came, he could go out as the kind of man he always thought himself to be.

A recent rain had made the Comanche's trail easy to follow, and the deep tracks created ruts as the mud dried in the sun. Jim wanted to tell himself that his enemy were just in too big of a hurry to stop and cover their tracks, but he couldn't help thinking that maybe John had been right about this whole thing being a trap.

His thoughts were interrupted by the shadow of something overhead. Looking up, he saw two buzzards circling up ahead about a hundred yards or so. Reining in his horse, Jim climbed from the saddle with his rifle in hand.

Approaching as carefully as he could in such an exposed position, he found the carcass of a calf. Jim chased off the four buzzards that were taking their turn picking the meat off its bones so that he could examine it more closely. From the condition of the carcass, it must have been killed four or five hours earlier. There was no sign that the meat had been cooked, and as most white men would never eat raw meat, it must have been butchered by the Comanche.

Jim chose a spot-on top of a little hill that offered a good view for about a mile in every direction. Jim could see no one in front of him, but behind him he could make out the dust cloud of an approaching rider. He could see no other area around that offered a better defensive position, so he decided to wait right where he was and find out if this rider was friend or enemy.

While he waited for the rider to arrive, Jim used the time to look for some water for himself and his horse. Where there were calves there were cows and where there were cows there was water, and it had to be close by.

Hidden at the bottom of a shallow draw, and obscured by tall prairie grass, Jim found a small pond. The rain runoff from the higher ground collected in the small cleft at the foot of the hill, forming a small muddy pond. The water had an alkaline smell due to the heavy minerals in the soil. While not as inviting as the clear springs of the Hill Country, the water was wet and best of all it was there.

After watering his horse and then drinking his fill, Jim waited in the semi-shade of the bluff. His position was hidden from the trail, allowing him to see anyone riding up, and they would be well within rifle range.

The sound of the horses' hooves on the hard ground could be heard even before the rider came into his field of view, and by the sound, they were approaching at a fast trot. Whoever it was, they weren't Indians, but the odds were they weren't up to any good either. Jim just wanted them to hurry up so he could get this business settled and get back on the trail. The day was turning hot, and he didn't plan on wasting all of it waiting around for some stranger, no matter what their intentions.

Jim had plenty of experience lying in wait for his prey. Long nights on guard duty, and cold mornings hunting deer, had taught him the art of silently waiting. The Sharps rifle was comfortably resting in the crook of his shoulder, with the barrel balanced on the palm of his free hand. While Jim wasn't the marksman that John was, he was still a pretty fair shot, and besides, at this distance he couldn't possibly miss.

He concentrated on controlling his breathing, so as not to move the rifle. The sun was hot on his back, and he could feel the first drips of sweat running down his face. He could hear the hooves of the approaching horse getting closer, and knew the rider would be coming into view any moment.

Jim would have only a second to decide if they were friendly or not; whether to shoot or let them ride on. He applied the slightest pressure to the trigger so all that would be required was to squeeze, and the fifty-caliber projectile would be sent down range on its mission of death.

Through the leaves of the cottonwood tree, he could see the rider come into view, but Jim could not make out his face. The rider was too far away to tell, but Jim was sure there was something familiar about him. Then Jim noticed the copper color of the horse's mane and he was sure the rider was Heck. Lowering the Sharps, he quickly jumped into the saddle and went to intercept his young pursuer.

"What the hell are ya doin' here, kid?" Jim said, wheeling his horse to a stop in front of Heck. "Do you realize I damn near shot you just now?"

Not knowing how close he had actually come to death, Heck said, "Sorry, Jim. I just didn't feel right letting you go after them alone, so I decided to come after you and help."

"You've got gumption, kid. I'll give ya that," Jim said, "but this is something I'm doing alone."

"Jim, I don't know much about Rangering, but I do know that if you go against them alone, they'll kill you," Heck said.

"Maybe, but that's my choice. If I stand a chance, I will have to move quick, without any hesitation. I won't

have time to look out for you, too. You'll make a good
Ranger one day, but right now, you'd just be in my way."

"I didn't ride all this way just to turn back, so unless
you wanna keep burning daylight, we'd better get moving,"
Heck said.

"You're right. With every minute we waste here, those
Comanche are getting further away, so I'll let you ride with
me. When it comes time to take them, you will hide
somewhere and let me do what has to be done. That's the
only way this will work. Do you agree?" Jim said.

Heck smiled, "Sure, Jim. Whatever you say."

"Your tone don't give a man much confidence, but I'll
take you at your word." Turning his horse, Jim led the way
and both men proceeded down the trail.

Chapter Fifteen

Freidrick and his siblings had been riding hard for hours. Their captors were pushing them hard since they broke camp early that morning, stopping only a few minutes to butcher and eat a calf. One of the braves tossed a bloody piece of meat in front of the children.

"I ain't eating that. It ain't even cooked," Eva said.

"Just eat it, Evie," Freidrick said. "We've got to keep our strength up, and we don't know when they'll feed us again."

"But it's all bloody. I can't do it, Freidrick," Eva said.

The Indians were sitting in a group a few yards from the children, and hearing Eva and Freidrick talking, they looked at them with utter contempt and hate.

"They're looking at us, Evie," Freidrick said. He grabbed the meat and took a big bite. As he ripped the flesh with his teeth, he suppressed the urge to puke up the raw meat. It had a metallic taste mixed with grass, and the congealed blood stuck in his throat as he quickly swallowed the putrid beef. "It ain't so bad once you get it in your mouth."

The other three tore into the meat and quickly chewed and swallowed. All three gagged as it went down, but their intense hunger won out over the horrible taste.

"I can't do this every day, Freidrick. We have to get away from here," Johannes said.

Wiping the blood from his mouth, Freidrick said, "We'll get away, but until we do, we have to do what we're told."

The excruciating pace was taking its toll on Eva, Carl, and Johannes. None of them had much riding experience and Freidrick was worried that if they couldn't keep up, the Indians would kill them like they had Rebecca. He wanted to offer words of encouragement to them, but he was afraid they would see through his lie, and that would make matters worse. The one opportunity they had to escape did not work out, and Freidrick was afraid to try again.

The previous night the party had camped in a clearing not far from a river, and when morning came, the Indians had left them alone with just one guard. The children were not bound and Freidrick thought they could easily get away.

The man guarding them was busy packing up the camp and not really watching them very closely. Freidrick had signaled for the others to start running for the trees, but before they could move, they heard gun shots off in the distance. It sounded like a horrible battle which caused their guard to stop what he was doing and cover them with his rifle. Before they had another chance to run, most of the others had returned and soon they were all racing down the trail like they were being chased by Lucifer himself.

The landscape had changed since they began their journey. They had started in the vast hills of South Texas, then crossed into the plains, and were now starting to enter the more wooded areas of northern Texas. The trees offered cover from the harsh summer sun, but Freidrick knew that the woods would offer cover for the Indians and make it harder for anyone to find them. They had crossed numerous creeks and small streams, but had not stopped for water. Freidrick could feel his throat tightening up from lack of water. He knew his lips were starting to blister as well, but he was more concerned about his siblings. Freidrick knew he could make it through whatever he had to in order to survive, but Carl, Eva, and Johannes were not as tough as he was. He knew he must find some way to get their captors to stop so the other children would have a chance to rest.

"Hey! When are we going to stop?" Freidrick said. "They need to stop and rest. They need water."

His pleas went unanswered from the stoic warrior. Freidrick could think of no other option, so he dug his heels into the horse's side and dove off as it started to gallop. Hitting the ground hard, he rolled a couple of times, made it to his feet, and started to run towards a small stand of trees about fifty yards away.

Freidrick had been deprived of both food and water for days and had not been able to walk much less run in that time. These factors made his making it to the trees highly unlikely, but that was not what was important.

He could feel the mounted Indian closing in on him. The sounds of the hooves were getting closer. Freidrick knew he wouldn't make it much longer, but he would hold out for as long as he could. The tree line was less than twenty-five yards away and Freidrick started to think that he might actually make it, when he felt a hand on his back and he was sent sprawling onto the ground.

He tried to make it back to his feet, but something hit him from behind. Another blow was delivered and then another. Through the pain Freidrick could tell that the Indian was hitting him with something hard. The Comanche rolled him over, yelling something in his language that Freidrick took to be some sort of insult. He tried to rise, but the Indian put his foot on his chest and continued to hurl Comanche insults at him. He moved his face to within an inch of Freidrick's and yelled at him while pointing to the other children. Freidrick could smell the scent of putrefied beef on the Comanche's breath as he spoke and felt the spray of spit as the Indian yelled in his face.

Freidrick leaned back and hocked a large wad of spit into the Indians face. For a second or two the Comanche couldn't believe what had happened. He just stared into Freidrick's eyes, a look of furry building into his gaze. Freidrick could see the hatred in the eyes of his captor and started to worry that maybe he had pushed him too far; that he might just kill him. The Indian stood up and pulled the hammer back on his rifle, leveling it at his head.

Freidrick looked at the man, wondering if he would really pull the trigger or not. He looked past the war paint, past the tanned features and looked straight into his soul. What he saw shocked him, but also frightened him more than the rifle that the man was pointing at him. He knew he would die.

"Hey! What's going on here?"

Fredrick and the Comanche turned in the direction of the voice and saw two men on horseback. The two riders were dressed in buckskin shirts and breeches, and carried hides and pelts across the back of a pack mule. They approached Freidrick and the Comanche with caution, both had shotguns in their hands.

The larger of the two spoke, "Well, look what we have here Clem, a bunch of damn thieving Indians and some children they stole. I'll bet we could get a nice reward for this bunch of savages and for bringing these kids back."

Laughing, Clem nodded in agreement. "Your right. We'll get a sight more than these damn hides we spent a week collecting."

The larger man stopped in front of Freidrick and the Comanche leader, who were both still on the ground, while Clem covered the rest of the Indians with his long barrel shotgun. Clem motioned for everyone to drop their weapons.

"All of ya'll throw your weapons over there. Come on now, I know you understand what I'm saying. Do it now!" He said.

"These damn ignorant savages are too stupid to know what's about to happen," the larger man said. "It don't matter, though. As soon as we collect their guns, let 'em have it."

Slowly, all of the Indians dropped their rifles, bows, and knives. None of the children moved a muscle. The younger children were more scared of these white men than they were of the Indians, but Freidrick was happy that these men came along. Otherwise, he knew he would have been dead. He recognized, however, that these were not good men, and figured they might kill him and his siblings as quick as the Comanche.

"Their scalps should bring us a fine price," Clem said with a grin. "Not to mention the stories we'll be able to tell. Hell, we won't have to buy our own drinks ever again," he laughed.

"What about these brats?" The larger man said.

"We'll kill them too," Clem said. "Without any witnesses, we can tell any story we want. Besides, I don't care about having to play nurse maid to this pack of brats anyhow."

The pair were so busy thinking about all the free whiskey their false tale would get them back in town, they had no idea how close to death they actually were.

Clem and his partner started collecting their newly acquired weapons; over confident in the ease of their conquest. What they did not see was the knife that one of the braves had hidden behind his back. One second of inattention was all it took.

The white men were concentrating on their spoils and not paying attention to their captives. Obviously, these men were not accustomed to fighting Comanche. With unbelievable quickness, the brave leapt forward, and drove the blade of his butcher knife through Clem's heart.

The larger man froze at the sight of his friend's death and didn't know what to do. He was used to killing his prey from hiding or in overwhelming numbers. He was not used to fighting hand to hand. Aware of the danger he was in, he tried to raise his shotgun, but it was too late.

The Comanche leader had picked up a thick tree branch and was on top of the big man before he could get off a shot. The Comanche clubbed the man in the head so many times his own mother would have been unable to recognize him. The whole band descended on the pair like a pack of dogs. They mutilated both bodies so badly it was difficult to even recognize the two as human.

Freidrick was still lying on the ground when the Indian approached him carrying the bloody branch he had used to beat the man. Freidrick said a quick prayer, knowing he was about to die, but he no longer felt afraid. He wasn't scared of dying, but he was afraid of dying like a coward.

He stood up and yelled at the Comanche. "Go on, do it! Kill me. I don't care. It's better than being taken to wherever you plan to take us. It's better than being eaten or being your slaves forever! So, go ahead and do it! That's all you savages know! Just kill me!"

The Comanche looked at Freidrick for a moment, tightening his grip on the tree branch. Then a slight smile came across his face and he motioned for Freidrick to get back on the horse.

Freidrick exhaled a long breath. He was very happy to be alive, and even happier that his plan had worked. His siblings had gotten a moment to rest, though he had not counted on the Comanche trying to kill him, or on the white men coming along. He felt sorry for the two men, but his plan had worked and his family was all still alive; at least one more day.

CHAPTER SIXTEEN

After dusk, the waxing moon provided enough light for the two Rangers to continue on the trail, but it would also make them inviting targets for anyone waiting along the way to ambush them. Every few miles they would stop while Jim checked for signs that they were still on the trail of the Comanche. The night was warm and muggy, and both Rangers were low on water; a condition which could lead to death in the Texas summer, even at night.

"We're gonna have to stop soon and look for water," Heck said, sipping the last of the brownish water from the bottom of his canteen. The water was gritty and it choked his throat going down, but to him it tasted like a drink from a cool stream.

"Yeah, I know," Jim said. He did not really want to take the time, but they would never find the Comanche or their captives if they died from thirst. "We'll go a few more miles and start looking. With the recent rain, it shouldn't be too hard to find some small ponds just off the trail."

The moonlight gave an eerie glow to the prairie and the grass seemed to dance in the summer breeze. Heck was having the adventure he had always dreamed of. He was hot on the trail of Indians, with danger around every corner, and sleeping underneath the stars. However, this wasn't exactly what he had in mind. He hadn't counted on thirst, and while they were underneath the stars, they weren't exactly sleeping. He tried not to think about the possibility that there could be Indians hiding in the tall grass just off the trail, ready to jump out and scalp them before they knew what was happening. To take his mind off everything, Heck decided to bring up something that had been bothering him.

"Who is Shaking Hand and why does he want to kill Rangers?" Heck Said.

The question caught Jim off guard. It hadn't occurred to him that Heck wouldn't have known about Shanking Hand or the history involved between him and the Rangers. Jim didn't really feel like talking, but he figured that if the kid was willing to risk his life, then he ought to know who his enemy was.

"I figured you had heard stories about Shaking Hand already," Jim said.

Heck just shook his head.

"Well," Jim said, "you've heard of Buffalo Hump, haven't you?"

Of course, Heck knew of Buffalo Hump. He was the scourge of Texas; the most famous of the Comanche chiefs.

Buffalo Hump was the Boogeyman that parents used in order to keep their young children in line. Every child living on the Texas frontier knew better than to wonder off too far from the house lest Buffalo Hump steal them and cook them in a stew. He had waged a scorched earth war against the white settlers for over twenty years.

"Of course, I've heard of Buffalo Hump," Heck said.

"Sorry kid," Jim said, "I forgot you've been raised on some of the same stories as I was. Well, Shaking Hand is married to Buffalo Hump's sister and he is every bit as bad as his brother-in-law; if not worse. He has robbed and murdered his way across Texas for years. He leads the Nokoni band and hates all White people. His warriors are ordered to kill all of the White adults and to capture all their children. If they can't make captives of the children, then they are to kill them as well. I guess Old Tom told you about the Friesen family."

Heck nodded, "Yes, he told me."

The sound of a coyote howling in the distance interrupted his narrative, and Jim remained silent until he assured himself that it was indeed a coyote. After a few moments, he continued, "We should have been able to get the Friesen children back. We just weren't prepared and had to give up. We let those Indians get away with taking those kids, and damned them to no telling what kind of hell. That stuck with me and I vowed I'd never let that happen again. Well, about three years ago, Shaking Hand sent a group of warriors out on a raid for supplies and captives. They raided several ranches along the Llano. They killed six German settlers and made off with cattle, horses, and four small children. I was part of the Ranger company that tracked them. We chased them for two weeks all the way to the Palo Duro Canyon before we caught up to them. We scouted their camp and found the children, but no braves. I figured we had really lucked out, and that the Comanche had abandoned the captives and just lit out. Boy, was I wrong." He paused here a moment to survey the trail ahead, but seeing nothing continued, "You see, the children were used as bait. We were led into a trap and we walked right into it. The Comanche had hidden in a small embankment that set about ten feet above their camp. We had no cover and no place to go. After that, they rode down on us like God's own vengeance. We stood our ground and gave as good as we got. It seemed like it went on for hours, but it couldn't have lasted for more than a few minutes. Afterwards, they rode off as quickly as they rode in, but not before we had killed two of 'em. We found out later that the two warriors we had killed were Shanking Hand's brother and his oldest son."

Not wanting to miss a word, Heck's gaze was fixed on the older Ranger. "What about the kids?" Heck said. "Were the kids, ok?"

Jim looked at the ground. "No, the Comanche had killed the captives before we arrived. They had just made it look like they were still alive to lead us into their trap."

Heck couldn't believe it. He thought he had heard all the stories about the Rangers, but he had never heard this one. "Did ya'll go after 'em?" Heck said, afraid that he was going to say something to make Jim mad.

"Who was gonna go after 'em, kid?" Jim said after taking a deep breath. "Henry and me was the only ones left. Out of ten Rangers, we was the only ones who made it out alive. Henry and me was shot up pretty good, so we buried our dead and made our way back to San Antonio."

Even after all these years, Jim still found it hard to talk about. "Since that day, all Shaking Hand cares about is killing Rangers. They say any brave who kills a Ranger gets half of everything taken in the raid. I guess it doesn't matter to him that they had killed eight Rangers. We had killed his son and brother, so now he's after blood." Jim reined his horse in and signaled for Heck to stop his horse. "You see kid, if we find them, it's going to be a slaughter. Either them or us. No prisoners. No quarter given. It'll just be kill or be killed. I'm sorry to say those children don't stand a chance. If they're not dead already, they will be as soon as the shooting starts."

Neither Ranger spoke for the rest of the night. The silence was broken only by the occasional screech of an owl, or the lonely howl of a coyote. As the first gentle rays of the sun peeked above the green sea of prairie grass, both men and horse were spent. They would be forced to make camp to rest.

In a small stand of trees about two hundred yards off the trail, the Rangers laid out their bed rolls. The trees provided cover from the trail and would shield them from the afternoon sun. Heck found a low lying rocky area at the bottom of a shallow crevice where the rain water collected. He filled up four canteens and lapped up all he could drink. He would have to come back later and refill all the canteens. By the time the midday sun hit, the little pond would dry up in a matter of hours. When Heck made it back to camp, Jim had a small fire burning and was in the process of cooking up some cornmeal cakes.

"Did you find any water?" Jim asked, looking up from the blazing fire.

"Yeah. There's a small pond about half a mile that way," Heck said, pointing in the direction from which he had just come. "It won't be there by night fall, so we'd better drink all we can."

Jim nodded, as he flipped the golden-brown cakes, "We'll fill up again before we head out. Do you think you can get some of that water on the fire for coffee? These cakes are almost done."

After eating their cornmeal cakes and washing it down with a cup of syrup-like chickaree coffee, the two Rangers laid down and prepared to get a quick rest. Jim grabbed his rifle. "We'll sleep in shifts. I'll take the first watch and wake you up in two hours. Keep your pistol close and I'll call out if I see anything."

Heck slept restlessly, due to the oppressive heat. He tossed and turned, jerking awake several times in the throes of nightmares about Indian attacks and being scalped. Eventually, though, he was carried away into an almost peaceful sleep, dreaming instead about home and fishing in the Perdernales with his father and brother. His mother was waiting to brag about her three men bringing home dinner. He and his brother were laughing at each other as only brothers can. Their father was feigning anger about the boys scaring the fish, but behind that there was an almost imperceptible smile that even two young children could recognize. It must have been late March or early April, a fine time of year in Texas, when the cool winds mixed with the warm sun to create a temperature that was perfect for fishing and just being outside and cutting up with your brother.

Atticus called out, "It's time to go home boys. Your mother will be about ready to start supper soon and we still have to clean all of these fish."

"Aw come on, Paw. Can't we stay a little while longer? The fish are still biting," Jefferson begged.

"No, we have to get back, and besides it's time for Heck to wake up," their father said, with a smile. Heck looked at his father confused. What did he mean it was time for him to wake up? His father never called him Heck, but always Jess.

"Wake up, Heck," His father repeated again. "Wake up, boy. Heck, it's your watch."

Heck realized it wasn't his father speaking. But who?

"Heck, get up. It's your watch." Heck woke with a shudder and set straight up to find Jim standing over him. Jim put his hand on his shoulder. "You alright, kid?"

Heck rubbed his eyes with the palm of his hand and stared at Jim, trying to remember where he was and what was going on. Jim patted him on the back.

"Damn kid, that must of been a good nap. Hey, it's your watch and I'm about dead on my feet. There hasn't been so much as a jack rabbit moving out there. Take the rifle and climb up that tree a few feet. You'll be able to see for several miles in every direction," he said, handing Heck the Sharps and pointing over his shoulder to a big oak tree about twenty yards from where they were standing.

Heck stood watch up in the old, oak tree for about two and half hours. He figured after everything, Jim deserved a little extra sleep. He kept alert by trying to figure out what they would do when they finally found the Comanche. He felt sure that Jim was right and they would not be able to just take the Indians by force without getting the child captives killed in the process. They would have to come up with some sort of plan and take the Indians by surprise, and that would be a problem. Sneaking up on a Comanche was impossible even for other Indians. He couldn't seem to come up with any idea that he felt had much of a chance of working, but he was certain that Jim would have a plan when the time came. That was the only thought that made Heck feel they had any hope at all; that Jim, with all his many years of experience, could come up with some sort of plan on the fly.

Heck climbed down and put another pot of coffee on the small fire. Feeling it might be some time before they would have a chance to make camp again, Heck figured they had better have another cup of coffee before hitting the trail. Heck also hoped the smell of the coffee would wake Jim up and save him the inevitable task of having to wake him up himself. He knew from experience that Jim always woke in a bad mood, even after the best night's sleep

CHAPTER SEVENTEEN

. After two days ride, the Rangers were just a few miles south of the Red River, the natural border between Texas and the Indian Territory. Heck knew that beyond the river, the Rangers had no legal authority, and the Comanche would have an infinite number of reinforcements.

Jim slowed his horse to a slow walk and put his finger to his lips, signaling Heck to be quiet.

"We need to be very quiet from here," Jim said, "We're going to head northeast for about a mile. There's a small canyon where I'll leave you with the horses and do a little scouting along the river."

Heck took a moment to think about what Jim had just said. "You don't think they've crossed over into Indian Territory?"

Jim was looking from the ground and then to the horizon. He started counting to himself; solving some equation that obviously meant something only to him.

"Hey, Jim. Did ya hear me?"

Jim rode off the trail heading northeast, but still at the same slow walk. With very thinly veiled irritation, Heck repeated his question.

"Jim, are you gonna answer my question or not?"

Jim stopped his horse and slowly turned around in his saddle. "Kid, I heard you the first time. I'm a little busy trying to figure out in what direction our friends went. They haven't crossed to the other side of the river. I've been tracking them and their tracks are no more than an hour old. They would not cross the river without watering their horses and getting a little rest for themselves. Just like us, they've been riding hard for two weeks and this is the only reliable water for the next two day's ride. There are about a hundred places to cross the river from here, so they could be almost anywhere. I'm going to search up and down the river by myself on foot. There are also about a hundred good places for an ambush along this part of the river. From here on out, you let me do the thinking and you try to keep quiet and just do what I say, and maybe we'll both get out of this alive. Is any part of what I've just said unclear?"

Heck quickly shook his head and motioned for Jim to lead the way.

Jim found the small canyon he had remembered and the two Rangers descended, single file, down a narrow path between two red dirt walls. The path was so narrow that both men's legs scraped the red clay walls on either side.

They descended about ten feet to the bottom, which then opened to a narrow crevice that ran parallel to the river and was concealed by rocky cliffs on both sides.

"I'll leave you here with the horses," Jim said, surveying the area. He was proud of himself for remembering this hiding place from years before, "Unless someone follows the trail down here, you'll never be seen." Jim noticed the look of uneasiness on the face of his companion. He found it easy to forget that Heck was really still a kid and not accustomed to the uncertainties of Rangering. "It'll be fine, kid. I'm going to scout the area and if I find them, I'll come up with a plan." Heck nodded and looked at Jim with an expression that he hadn't seen on the face of his young companion before. It was a look of fear.

Heck didn't want to admit that he was afraid, not even to himself, but the closer they got to overtaking their enemy the more he could feel the tightening in his stomach. His palms were sweating and he could feel his heart racing. These were symptoms that Heck was not familiar with, but ones that he knew could only be caused by fear. He knew the eventual conclusion of this pursuit would be a great battle, but that's not what really had him scared.

What worried Heck the most was that when it really counted, he would not be there for Jim; that he would be unable to do his part. All he had ever wanted to be was a Texas Ranger and what happened in the next hour would tell the story of whether he had what it took. He figured it would be best to put these thoughts out of his head and just stick to the job at hand.

"So, what happens when you do find them?" Heck said, forming his fears into this one simple question.

Jim looked at him and almost smiled, "Well, I'll come back here to get you and we'll come up with some kind of plan. Just remember that in battle, the plan usually lasts for about a minute before things change and then the plan goes right out the window. The most important thing to remember is to keep a cool head and rely on your instincts. Once the fighting starts, things will happen very fast, just like when we were attacked back on the Brazos. You did fine there. You did what you had to do as things happened and you made it out alive. You'll do the same thing here. Like I said, just keep your head. Nine times out of ten the man that stays calm and doesn't panic is the one who walks away from the fight. Now I'm gonna go and see what I can find and you stay here and wait. If I'm not back in one hour, get the hell outta here as fast as you can and don't look back."

Heck realized that one man would be more effective at scouting than two, but if things went bad, there was no way he was just going to leave Jim here. "I'll wait here for you, but if you aren't back in an hour, I'm coming after you," Heck said.

Jim grabbed Heck by the shoulder. "Kid, if I'm not back in an hour, it means I'm done for and you need to save yourself. They'll realize that I'm not alone and they'll start looking for ya. You won't have much chance of escape, but maybe you'll get lucky."

Heck knew that Jim was probably right, but he chuckled and stuck out his hand. "You sure look on the gloomy side of things." Both men laughed, shook hands, and then parted ways.

CHAPTER EIGHTEEN

The sun had set beyond the walls of the small canyon by the time Heck started to get worried. He was sure it had been more than an hour since Jim had left to scout the Comanche position, and it was time for him to make a decision.

There was really no decision to make, Heck was not going to leave his friend behind and he sure wasn't going to let the Comanche escape with their captives. He decided to follow Jim's path as far as he could and from there he would have to rely on the skills he had been taught. Luck would have to carry him the rest of the way.

He followed the canyon trail for about a mile upstream before it started ascending back up. He crawled on his belly the last few feet to the top and carefully stuck his head out to survey the terrain. He was about ten feet above the river, which was about fifty yards away, and he found signs that someone had recently slid down the bank. He doubted Jim would have attempted a river crossing here since it offered no cover. Heck decided he would slide down the bank and make his way along the tree line, which ran parallel with the river for as far as the eye could see. It was almost dark and he thought he had a pretty good chance of making the tree line without being seen.

The bank was about a forty-five degree slope and luckily was mostly red dirt with very few rocks, so he was able to reach the bottom quickly and rather painlessly. Once at the bottom, he ran as fast as he could, but the red dirt was wet, which created a bog like surface that his feet sunk into with every step. Running in this muck was impossible, so he half walked half crawled, pulling his feet out with a sucking sound every step of the way. If anyone was within ear shot of his position, they would already know he was there, so he pushed his way through the red bog as quickly as he could; not worrying about stealth, just trying to make the trees as quickly as possible.

Out of breath and with his legs aching from the fifty-yard dash through the red clay bog, Heck collapsed behind a large cottonwood tree. He peered from around the sides of the tree to see if anyone was moving along the river, or if there was any sign that he had been detected. He saw nothing, but that offered little comfort. The Comanche could be descending down on him this very moment and he would never know it.

Looking in every direction, Heck decided his best option was to continue heading up river. There was no sign that anyone had been through that bog except him recently, but he felt sure that Jim had headed up river and he would have used these woods as cover the same as he had.

Coming out from his hiding place, he crept through the woods. Going from tree to tree, he stopped for a second each time to look and listen for anything unusual. Hearing only the sound of birds and the occasional cricket, he continued moving. Old Tom was still repeating in his ear, "Look for things out of the ordinary. Silence where there should be noise. Birds taking flight all of a sudden. Always pay close attention to your surroundings." It wasn't a sound that drew his attention, but a smell. The smell of fire.

Heck followed the smell for about a half mile to a small clearing on the edge of the woods. He was careful where he put his feet so as not to make any noise and give away his position. He knew he would have to come up with some sort of plan, but at the moment he had no idea what that would be.

He counted five braves in the camp, although he knew it was probable that there were one or two more that he did not see. Heck found the captives sitting in the middle of camp. They appeared to be okay, but he had not forgotten Jim's story about how the Comanche would use captives as a trap.

There were two lean-tos on the edge of camp, made from tree branches and brush, and enclosed on three sides. Judging from their appearance, they were hastily constructed, but Heck had to admire the ingenuity of the Comanche. He couldn't see inside, so he decided to assume there were several more within.

There was a trail leading down to the river where the Comanche probably had their horses tied. Heck didn't see any sign of Jim. Had he been captured, he would have certainly seen him in the camp. If he had been killed, there should have been some sign of his body. The Comanche didn't seem to be on guard, the campfire proved that.

Heck couldn't understand what the Comanche were saying, but they did not appear agitated. He thought he might take them by surprise, but the odds were at least five to one against him. Even if by some miracle he did kill them all, the captives would be caught in the crossfire. The one thing he did have going for him was the Comanche's campfire, as it illuminated their whole camp while obscuring the surrounding woods. He believed he would be well hidden as long as he didn't make any noise. He figured the best option for now was to fall back deeper into the woods and try to formulate his plan.

The woods were in complete darkness now. Even the faint light emitted from the sliver of moon was blotted out by the thick canopy above his head. He decided to wait until the Comanche went to sleep and then attack. They would surely have several guards posted, but he hoped he might be able to sneak up on them before the rest of the camp was alerted.

The night was still, and there was hardly a breath of wind, so the sound of rustling leaves instantly drew his attention. It was more than likely an animal of some sort, but his gut was telling him something else. He was trying to decide where the noise came from when an arm grabbed him from behind and a hand covered his mouth.

The Comanche were known to sneak up on their enemies and slit their throats, but fortunately this was no Comanche. His attacker's voice put him instantly at ease.

"Take it easy, kid. It's me, Jim," he whispered.

Heck turned around and faced his friend.

"I thought I told you to get outta here if I didn't come back."

Heck could detect a strain in his friend's voice, and a grimace on his face. "What happened to you? Why didn't you come back?"

Jim knelt down, and Heck saw that he was favoring his left leg, which was splinted. "Your leg. Is it broken?" Heck said.

"Yes, I believe it is," Jim answered, placing his hand on the wounded appendage. "It was stupid really. Wasn't watching where I was going and stepped into a pit. It was probably dug as a trap. The problem is that I can barely walk, much less take on five Comanche. This mission is over kid. You need to get outta here. I'll give you time to get to your horse before I move in. You might just be able to make it out before they kill me. It's your best chance for survival. You need to take it."

"Your plan is to die here and let those kids die as well?" Heck said. "We can still save them. Let me go in and get them out."

Jim smiled. He was impressed with his young friend, but he couldn't help but laugh at the thought of this kid leading a rescue all by himself. "You kid? You're gonna go in there all by yourself and bring those children out alive? I admire your gumption kid, but it's suicide. You get outta here and—"

"Listen to me," Heck interrupted. "I'll remove the guards and get the captives out. You'll take up a position from the woods covering the camp and kill the others if they wake up. They'll be groggy and not ready for a fight. We'll be taking them by surprise. Look, I realize it's not a great plan, but it's got a chance of working and maybe getting those children back home alive. A small chance is better than no chance at all."

"Ok kid, you win," Jim said. "We'll do it your way."

There was only one Comanche guarding the children, and he was sitting with his legs crossed, facing them. Heck would be exposed for only a moment before reaching the Indian, but the captives would see him coming. If they stirred in any way, the guard would be apt to turn around and the plan would be over.

Heck crept along the edge of the camp, careful not to step on any twigs or rustle the leaves underneath his feet. The night was still and any noise at all would surely give away his presence. The beating of his own heart seemed to echo through the night like a drum; its cadence keeping time with each measured step. Coming up behind the lean-tos, he could hear the snores of the others as they slept, hopefully muffling the sounds of his footsteps which otherwise might have been audible to the trained ear of the Comanche.

Heck took a moment, still in the cover of the trees, to survey the scene. He could detect no movement; the sentry was still in place with his back turned to him. He would have to cross a distance of at least fifteen feet in the open to reach his target without making a sound, or having the children make any movement that would arouse the suspicion of their guard. He held his breath, imagining that the sound of his breathing and the very pounding of his heart was audible to the whole camp.

The Comanche were believed by some to possess the ability to sense the presence of their enemies. In the light of day, Heck knew this was a myth meant to strike fear into the hearts of their enemies, but here, in the darkness, it seemed perfectly plausible that this mysterious people, so connected to nature and so adept in battle, could sense the presence of someone so out of balance with their surroundings. The longer he knelt in the perceived safety of the woods, the more Heck could feel his nerves failing him; his own mind defeating his mission. Heck rose to his feet and stealthily crept into camp. His eyes were fixed on the back of the Comanche before him. He could see the man's shoulders rise and fall with each breath, his hair tied neatly in a braid stretching to the middle of his back. The children sat still, as if afraid to make a move, their eyes wide open, but not seeing anything around them other than the threatening figure of the one guarding them. Heck quickly closed the distance to his intended target. He was no longer concerned with silence, just with reaching him before the Indian sensed the danger descending on him.

Within two feet of his prey, Heck stretched out his arm. His hand tightly gripped the stag handle of his bowie knife, and he quickly reviewed his plan of attack. The children were staring at him, but Heck could not be sure that they even perceived what was about to happen. They saw him, but at the same time seemed to look right through him. Without moving his head, the gaze of the oldest boy met his and suddenly there was a look of acknowledgement in the boy's grime crusted face. It was a look of relief mixed with fear. The Indian must have noticed the expression on the boy's face at the same moment Heck did, for he started to stand and turn around, but it was too late. Heck threw an arm around the man's head, jerking it back, and with the other hand made a fluid motion from left to right cutting deep into the Comanche's neck.   Heck could feel him struggle for just a moment before his body went limp, and he gently eased him to the ground; mindful not to make any sudden movements that would draw attention to his presence. Placing a finger to his lips, he signaled for the children to be quiet while he carefully cut their ropes. "My name's Heck and I'm a Texas Ranger. Just be quiet and follow me and you'll be home before you know it." Heck quietly led the four children to where he had left Jim.

CHAPTER NINETEEN

"Good job, kid. You did it," Jim said, as Heck and the children made it back to the woods. "Now get the kids back to the horses and get the hell out of here."

"No, Jim," Heck said. "We're all going out together."

"We don't have time for any argument," Jim said. "Those Comanche are going to start pouring out of there on us any minute. The only chance those children have is someone staying here and covering you while you get to the horses. I can't run, not with this leg, so I'm gonna stay here and play this out."

"But Jim—"

"I don't want to hear what you have to say. Just go. Don't look so glum, kid," he said pleasantly. "You done good. Now get outta here, and that's an order."

Heck wanted to say something. He knew he should say something. But what? He knew Jim was right. Getting the kids back was the mission and he had to finish it. He stuck his hand out and shook the hand of the man, who more than any other, had taught him what it really meant to be a Texas Ranger. For that, he would never forget him.

Heck grabbed the girl and then turned to the others and said, "Ok, on the count of three, I'm gonna start running and ya'll need to follow me and run as fast as you can. Do you understand?" All of the children nodded that they understood.

"Ok. Good. One, two, three." Heck and the four children disappeared into the darkness.

Jim pulled out his pistol and laid it on the ground next to him. He then loaded his rifle, feeling he was ready for what would come next.

Jim expected the Indians to start pouring out of the camp at any time, but nobody was stirring at all. He thought about just walking in and shooting them while they slept, but regardless of what they had done, he wasn't a murderer. The question about what to do next, however, was decided for him.

A pack of coyotes howling in the distance woke the camp, causing one of the Indians to step outside to investigate. The warrior had only taken a few steps out of the lean-to when a shot from Jim's Sharps rifle knocked him to the ground.

Setting the rifle on the ground, Jim picked up his pistol and waited for the others to emerge, but no one else came out. He decided to change positions to get a look into the lean-tos. Pulling out his other pistol, he limped forward. He had taken only about half a step when he felt a terrible burning in this left leg. He cried out in pain and fell to the ground.

Looking down, he saw an arrow protruding from his left leg, and about twelve inches of the wooden shaft was visible. Running his hand along the back of his leg, he felt the sharp head of the arrow sticking out about three inches on the other side. Without taking aim, Jim started pouring fire into the camp, but judging from the arrows raining down next to him, he knew his bullets were not finding their mark.

Once both guns were empty, Jim reached into his pocket and pulled out two replacement cylinders. It would take only seconds to reload, but this would give them plenty of time to descend on his position.

Five braves emerged, letting loose a volley of bullets and arrows on Jim's position, but surrender was not an option. He would make it a fight, regardless of the bleak chances of success.

Crawling on his stomach, he moved slowly; painfully. He made his way behind a large oak. It offered little protection, but it was the best option available. Poking his head out from behind the tree, Jim could see that the campfire had been doused and the camp was shrouded in total darkness.

"Smart move," Jim thought to himself. "That's what I would have done."

His eyes quickly adjusted to the darkness, and he was able to make out the silhouettes of several men, who were four or five yards away at most.

"It's now or never," Jim thought, as he made his move. Stepping out from behind the tree, fire belched from both barrels. He saw the black form of one of the figures fall to the ground. His other shot had apparently missed its mark. Jim continued firing, as the remainder of the Comanche started making their way forward; shooting as they moved. Ducking behind another tree, Jim slid to the ground. The end was at hand.

"Lord, they say you look out for drunks and fools. Well, I ain't what you'd call a drunk, but as for the other, I reckon an argument could be made. In the next second you're either gonna give me a miracle or welcome me home. Amen."

Crouching down, Jim crept from behind the tree, firing both pistols until he heard both hammers hitting on empty chambers. He then lowered his hands and let both guns fall to the ground.

Looking up, he saw the painted warriors standing over him. Looking into their eyes, he saw nothing that offered any hope of mercy. In them, he saw only death.

The expected sounds of gunshots rang out almost immediately, but what did not occur was the feeling of pain or the veil of death. Jim opened his eyes and looked at his foe, both men stood still for just a moment and then staggered forward, before falling at his feet.

With satisfaction, Heck saw that both of his shots found their mark.

"There's still one or two more of 'em out there," Jim said, sticking out his hand. "Help me up and let's get after 'em. You'd better loan me one of your pistols. Mine are both empty."

Heck helped Jim to his feet.

"I don't see any sign of 'em," Jim said. "You take the right and I'll take the left. Maybe we can trap them in between."

Heck nodded his agreement and started in the direction Jim indicated. Making his way in the darkness, he strained to see. He tried to make out the sound of footsteps in the soft, damp ground, but there was nothing. He thought about the children, and hoped they would remain hidden in the little ravine where he had left them.

The odds were even at two against two, but that offered little comfort. Heck knew that two Comanche were as good as at least five ordinary men, and in the darkness, they held the definite advantage.

Stopping to listen, he could hear only the sound of the wind rustling the trees overhead. He started to take a step when the sound of crunching leaves stopped him in mid stride. Directly in front of him stood a Comanche warrior with a pistol pointed at his chest. From behind him, he heard the sound of a hammer being cocked. He looked over his shoulder and saw another Indian ready to shoot him from behind. Heck drew a long, slow breath.

Over the course of the last few weeks on the trail, he had plenty of time to imagine this moment, and how he would face death when it came to claim him. In his imagining, he figured it would come as a surprise just like it said in the Good Book, "like a thief in the night," but apparently he was meant to look death in the eye; to see it coming. Faced with it, Heck wasn't really sure what to do. He knew he would never have time to raise his pistol before his enemy fired, so he decided the best thing to do was meet death on its own terms. He knew his knife was within reach. He would certainly be killed, but he might at least be able to take one of them with him. That would leave only one more for Jim to take care of.

Heck carefully lowered his hand, finding the handle of his knife, and he took one last breath.

In a single motion, he drew his knife, dropped to one knee, and hurled the bowie forward, embedding the blade in the Indians chest.

Taking careful aim, Jim pulled his hammer back, lined up his sights, and fired. In the blink of an eye, Jim could see that his shot struck the Comanche in the back of the head.

Heck let out a deep sigh, "I was beginning to wonder if you would ever fire," Heck said, with a wave to his friend. "Another second and I'd been joining these Indians in the hereafter."

Jim limped forward to join his young friend, "How did you know I was back there?"

Heck bent down and retrieved his knife from the dead Comanche, "Well, that's easy, Jim. I knew you weren't in front of me, and you wouldn't leave me here to face two Indians by myself, so you had to be behind me. Though, I didn't think it would take you so long to fire."

Jim slapped him on the back. "Look who's being hard to please all of the sudden. When we get back to San Antone, I might need to talk to Old Tom about having you clean the horse stalls for the next month to teach you some respect for your elders."

Heck looked down at his fallen enemy, and it seemed strange to him. This was the first time he had been able to look into the face of someone he had killed. The face looking back at him was that of a young man the same age as himself. His features even seemed similar, not as harsh as what Heck had imagined in his mind. In a different time, this boy and Heck might have even been friends.

Jim staggered to Heck's side. Looking down at the dead Indian, his gaze immediately fell on the young man's face. For a long moment, the Ranger stared at the dead

Indian. A shudder ran through the Ranger and he stumbled back a step, almost losing his footing altogether. Heck reached out a hand to steady his friend.

Heck turned to Jim, "He can't be more than fifteen or sixteen."

"He's seventeen, actually," Jim replied, still staring down at the young Comanche. "His name is Clinton Friesen. Do you see the half-moon scar on his cheek? He got that from falling off his horse into a fence post when he was eight. He's the boy I told you about. He was taken almost ten years ago."

Heck shook his head, trying to make some sense of what Jim had just said, but he couldn't. "I don't understand," Heck said. "Why would he kill his own people? I don't get it, Jim."

Jim turned and walked away, "It's more common than you think, kid. I've seen it before. These kids get taken and while we try to find them we're not always able to. They either adapt to life with the Indians or they die. A lot of them do die, but others come to see the Indians as their new family. They become part of the tribe and count on them for survival. We tried to save that boy, but we just weren't able to. It looks like he made a pretty good brave. He went from a nice kid to a cold-blooded killer in just a few years." He looked down at the boy once more and let out a deep sigh. "There's nothing that can be done about it now, kid. Go check on the children while I bury him. He was born a Christian and he should be buried as one."

CHAPTER TWENTY

Walking into the Ranger barracks, wearing a huge grin, Heck called out to Jim. "Hey old man, ya still laying around?"

Jim sat up in bed and gave his young comrade a heart wave. "Did you come in here just to give me grief?"

Heck pulled up a chair by the bed. "Naw, I just came to tell you that since you're taking it easy, the rest of us ar having to work extra hard." Heck took a seat in the chair b Jim's bed. "The Captain just made me a corporal and is sending me out on patrol first thing in the morning."

Jim roared with laughter. Laying back in bed he gave Heck a smack on the back. "Well things really must be in sorry state since I've been laid up."

Heck smiled and started to stand, but Jim motioned for him to remain seated. His demeanor suddenly took on a more serious tone. Heck nodded to signify that he was ready to hear whatever it was that he wanted to say. Jim reached under his bed and pulled out a bottle and poured whiskey into two glasses that were on the night table.

In a serious tone, Jim said, "I wanted to tell you that you did a good job out there, and I'd be proud to ride with you anytime."

Heck, with a slightly embarrassed smile started to speak, but Jim put up his hand to signal that he was not finished.

"You remind me a lot of myself not so many years ago, and that is both a good and a bad thing. We got real lucky out there, kid. We both could have easily died, and you need to think on that some. Life means something and I want you to always remember that. I watched you in battle and there was a single-minded fury that seemed to take over. You thrived in the heat of the fight and you didn't back down for nothin' or nobody. I used to be exactly like that back in my younger days. I lived for the fight, and I got to where I would go out looking for it. In battle, that quality can keep you alive, but you gotta be able to live after the fight is over. You'll want a normal life one day. A life that doesn't include fighting and living on the trail like some wild animal. I taught you how to use that gun, and you learned real well, but I taught you so you could save lives; your life as well as other people. I didn't teach you so you would make a life out of killing. I can tell you from experience that is no life at all. Do you get what I'm telling ya?"

Heck looked at his friend with a serious expression and paused before replying, "I understand what you're saying."

Jim smiled and poured them both another drink. "Good. That badge looks good on you kid, but don't ever forget what it stands for. Texas is going to be a great state one day, but it's gotta have law and order, and that's what we're here for."

CHAPTER TWENTY-ONE

1861

"What do you think this is all about?" Heck said, with a yawn.

"I don't know kid," Jim said, "but I promise you, it ain't good. The Captain don't ever want to talk to anybody this early."

"Well, I can tell you this," Heck said, "I don't like getting raised out of a warm bed at the crack of dawn without so much as a reason why."

"Maybe if you hadn't stayed out so late courtin' Ms. Rachel, you would be in a better mood this morning," Jim said, trying his best to irritate his friend. Joshing Heck was

Jim's favorite way to start the day, especially when Heck was easily riled from lack of sleep.

Joking aside, Jim couldn't have been prouder of the man Heck had grown into. In the nine years since Heck had first begged to join the Rangers, he had proven himself in countless engagements and never shirked his duties. He was a tenacious fighter and courageous pursuer of those who threatened the peaceful existence of his fellow Texans.

Under Jim's instruction, Heck had also become the deadliest gun hand he had ever seen; himself included. More pleasing to the older Ranger, though, was the wisdom and patience that he had always shown. Heck would always use his brain and common sense first, and was always happier when he could bring in a live prisoner. Jim thought that Heck might be the ablest Ranger in the company, and that was the best compliment he could give to anyone. Of course, he would never tell Heck that.

"I hope we have the afternoon free," Heck said earnestly. "I promised to take Rachel for a buggy ride later. If I can't make it, she will go with that fool Willard."

"Well it might be bad luck for you, but good luck for her," Jim said.

"What do you mean by that?" Heck said, more than a little hurt by his friend's remark.

Jim held back a grin and said, "I mean Willard is apt to be a big man someday. He has a good job at the bank, and word is he will make president within a few years. Anyone he chooses to marry will have a grand life. What can you offer her? Men like us are likely to die without leaving even enough money for the funeral."

"Talking to you is darned depressin', Jim," Heck said. "I'll tell you one thing, I don't plan on dying broke. I'm gonna be a rich land owner one day, and I'll amount to more than that idiot Willard."

"How do you plan on doing that?" Jim said, unable to suppress his laughter any longer.

Heck thought for a moment, but unable to think of anything simply said, "I don't have it all figured out yet, but I will. I promise you that."

"Well just don't forget about your friend Jim when you do. I figure I'm owed at least half your stake just for putting up with you for all these years," he said.

Walking into Captain Hale's office, the two Rangers were surprised to see a stranger sitting across the desk from the Captain. The stranger was older than Hale, but had the look of someone who could still get the job done. He was of average height with a strong build, and when standing, Heck thought he would cut a most imposing figure. The man had sandy blonde hair, with hints of gray around his temples. His weathered face was partially hidden behind a long handlebar mustache, which was also peppered with gray. The black suit he wore had only one distinguishing feature; there was a Texas Ranger's badge pinned to it.

"C'mon in and have a seat, boys," the Captain said in his usual somber tone. "Heck. Jim. This is Captain Ben McCullough of Company B." Captain McCullough stood up and shook each man's hand, pausing a moment with each, as if sizing them up.

Sitting back down, Captain Hale proceeded to explain why he had called them in so early. "Gentlemen, we've got an important assignment for you, and possibly your last as Texas Rangers." The Captain paused a moment to let these words sink in.

Jim and Heck looked at each other with astonishment and confusion, unable to understand why the captain would say such a thing.

"Captain," Heck said. "What do you mean our last mission? What is it you want us to do? What's going on?"

Captain McCullough removed a leather case from the breast pocket of his coat, and took out a cigar the size of a tree branch. Motioning for Captain Hale to get on with the explanation, he bit off the end of the cigar and lit it. McCullough was obviously a man accustomed to having others follow his commands, but Heck found it oddly discomforting to see Captain Hale being deferential to anyone.

Clearing his throat, Captain Hale set back in his chair and explained, "As both of you are aware, there have been rumblings of succession and it appears the Texas legislature has voted to do just that. We have left the Union and are joining the Confederacy. Governor Houston argued to the last against succession, but in the end, he was unsuccessful. Rather than take a position in the new government, he has chosen to resign; effective immediately. General Twiggs, the commanding general of all Texas forts, has surrendered them to the Confederacy, and the US troops have already begun evacuating." The Captain looked at both men, trying to judge what they were thinking, but mostly he wanted to get a hint of where their loyalties lay.

Neither Jim nor Heck spoke, they were both to shaken to utter a word. In a moment, the whole world had turned upside down, and the future of all they valued was suddenly in the balance. Captain Hale sympathized with what they were feeling; it was the same plight that people all over the South would be struggling with. They had gone to bed as Americans and were waking up in a new country with an uncertain road ahead. He wished he could give them longer to absorb what was taking place, but events were pressing them all forward; whether they wanted to go or not. They were all caught in the same maelstrom sweeping the whole nation towards war.

Captain McCullough impatiently moved his cigar from one hand to the other, doing his best to remain silent and let his fellow Captain explain the situation to his men. He was not unmoved by the gravity of these events or the way they would affect everyone involved, but there were things that needed to be done and a strict time frame in which to accomplish them. Rising from his chair, he felt it imperative to move things along. He took a long drag on his cigar and then began to speak, "Gentlemen, regardless of the political and governmental aspects of our current situation, you are still Texas Rangers, and as such you are expected to act in the best interests of this state. As Captain Hale stated, General Twiggs has surrendered all forts, and more importantly for our purposes, the arms contained within them. I am preparing to lead a cavalry company up to Missouri to stem the flow of abolitionists who want to spread their poison from Kansas into Missouri and presumably on into Arkansas and eventually Texas. They are murdering law abiding Southern sympathizers all along the border and must be stopped. To that end, we need the small arms and cannon currently secured within the walls of Fort Brown. Your mission will be to act as guides for a detachment of regular army and travel to the fort and return with the guns. I fear word of the surrender has already gotten out, and it won't take long for some bandit to get up the gumption to make a play for one of the forts. Fort Brown's position so close to the border makes it an ideal target for a raid from Mexico. The main body of the army stationed there has already evacuated, leaving only a very small contingent of men to handle the formal aspects of the transfer, and as you can imagine, if confronted, they will not be much motivated to put up a resistance. In short, time is of singular importance, so you will move out today and return with the weapons and artillery post haste. They will be stored in the armory at the Alamo until they can be distributed to the newly formed Confederate Cavalry."

Jim did not care for McCullough, and he did not particularly care for the idea of Texas throwing in with the Confederacy. He did, however, agree with McCullough on one point. They were still Texas Rangers and duty bound to follow orders.

Trying to conceal his dislike for the Captain, he said, "We will, of course, do our duty and retrieve the guns and return them to San Antonio, but what will happen then?"

"Well, Corporal King," McCullough said, "I need good men to help me stop this Jayhawker rabble, and I would be happy to have as many Texas Rangers as I can get. That, however, is a discussion for another time. Right now, we need those guns. Men will not be of much use without arms and artillery. Well, gentlemen, I will leave it to Captain Hale to go over the few particulars with you. The soldiers you are to be escorting will be waiting for you at your livery. Good day, gentlemen and God speed. Captain Hale, thank you for your assistance. Those of us going off to fight this scourge will sleep better knowing you are staying here to protect our great state." Snuffing out his cigar under his boot heel, Captain McCullough walked out of the office.

Captain Hale poured three cups of coffee from the pot percolating on the stove and handed a cup to each of the Rangers. Slowly, he sipped his coffee, taking a moment to choose his words carefully. "Boys, this mission is the start of what I believe will be a long and bloody conflict. There are some who believe war will never come, and that Lincoln will simply allow the South to secede without a fight. There are others who know a fight's coming, but are so full of their own self-importance that they think the South will easily beat the North. They are both full of hogwash. The North can field an army of over three million, and the South will be lucky to recruit one million. Even if the Confederacy can pull together an army of that size, they don't have the resources to equip even half that many. The Yankees have most of the factories and railroads; plus a navy. They can move men and material with ease wherever they want to. The South has the best generals and men willingly fighting for their homes, so they will put up a strong fight for a while, but it will just be dragging out the inevitable. In the end, the North will bottle them up in a few states, move the whole of the Union Army in to position and crush them to dust in one fell swoop."

"What are you saying, Captain?" Heck said, shocked by what he had heard.

"I'm saying that it doesn't matter how hard a fight the South puts up; the North will win. Lincoln has sworn to preserve the Union whatever the cost, and since his nickname is "Honest Abe," I imagine we can take him at his word. Many will die in the war, and they will die for nothing. I'd hate to see you boys get mixed up in a hopeless cause. You boys will be given a choice. You can either join the army or stay with the Rangers. We will be combining the existing Ranger companies into two, Companies A and C. I will be commanding Company C, which will be stationed along the Rio Grande to defend against any incursions by the Mexicans. I will need men that I can trust; ones that I already know and that know me. I hope you choose to stay with the Rangers and fight for your true home, Texas. Anyway, the choice will be yours, but you'll have a place with me anytime."

The Captain paused a moment to take another sip from his coffee cup. There was much he wanted to say to these men whom he had come to respect, but as often is the case when events are spiraling out of control, there simply wasn't enough time.

Captain Hale shook their hands and said, "I want you to take Tommy with you. You'll need someone to look after the horses and to act as messenger if you run into trouble. He's green, but no more than both of you were when you first came here. I know men and you will be able to count on him to do whatever needs doing. I have explained all of this to Corporal Curtis, and as senior man, he will be in charge on this mission. I wish we could afford to send more men with you, but there's no way to get Corporal Hagen or the others back from El Paso in time. I've seen these soldiers that you will be escorting, and I must say, I wasn't impressed by what I saw. They are filled with ideas of glory and the greatness of their cause. Three of them are farmers and one was a clerk in a dry goods store, and it is my opinion that they will collapse in the face of the enemy. Your job is to act as guides and nothing more. Do your best for them, but they are responsible for themselves. That's all I have to say. Just do what needs to be done and get back here."

After retrieving their gear, Jim and Heck entered the livery and saw Bob speaking with four men. Three of the men were quite tall and gangly looking, and wore clothes that they had outgrown some time ago. They were dressed in pretty much the same fashion of ill-fitting breeches, shirts whose holes were covered by homemade patches, and shoes which were really nothing more than a few pieces of old leather held together by minimal stitching.

The fourth man, whom Heck pegged immediately for the shopkeeper, was a good six inches shorter than his companions, but was considerably better outfitted. His trousers, while not expensive, fit perfectly, and along with the high collar linen shirt, gave him the appearance of someone accustomed to easy living. Jim and Heck agreed instantly with the Captain's impression of their charges.

"The horses are saddled and ready to go," Tommy said, poking his head through the barn door, "and I've loaded all the supplies on the two pack horses."

"Good job, kid," Jim said with a wave, "We'll be ready to ride in a minute."

Bob called both Jim and Heck over and introduced the four soldiers. "Jim. Heck. I want you to meet our comrades in arms for the next few weeks. This is Clel, Daniel, Cotton, and Mathias. They are privates in the new Confederate Army. Boys, this is Corporal Heck Carson and Corporal Jim King, and the three of us along with Tommy, who you've already met, will be escorting you to Fort Brown. It's going to be a hard trip, so we best get moving."

Heck suddenly ran to the door as if he had forgotten something very important. "I almost forgot. There is something I've got to do before we leave. I'll meet ya'll at the horses in a jiffy," he said running out the door.

As Heck entered the eating house, owned by the Lindsay family, he immediately spotted who he was looking for. "Rachel," he said, over the voices of the noisy patrons. "Rachel, come here."

"What are you doing here?" she said, more than a little surprised to see him. "I thought we weren't going riding until this afternoon."

Heck had his head hung low as if he were bringing more devastating news than merely a broken promise. "Well, uh, I uh, have some bad news," he said. "I have to go out on Ranger business and I don't really know when I'll be back. I'm awfully sorry, but this came up sudden like, and I gotta go."

"What!" she said, "You mean to tell me that you're breaking the plans that we've had for a week so you can go off on some dang fool mission with your friends."

Heck looked around and saw that all eyes were on the them, as if waiting impatiently for the next word. They seemed to take it as an entertaining distraction from their normal routine. Glaring back at the customers, he said, "Ya'll just go back to your food. This ain't no business of yours." Turning his attention back to Rachel he said in a calmer tone, "I'm real sorry, but I got no choice. What we're doing is real important. I'll be back as soon as I can and we'll go on that ride just like I promised."

"Just you forget it, Mister Carson. There's others around here who would gladly share company with me, so you do what you gotta and so will I."

A voice called out across the room, "Rachel dear. Is there something wrong?"

"No Momma," she said, "I was just telling this gentleman that we're all filled up and won't be able to help him after all."

Rachel's mother glared at Heck, the way only mothers can, and then said, "Well if that's all, you'd better get back to work. We've got paying customers to wait on here."

"I'm coming Momma. Good day, Mister Carson," she said, and with a flip of her hair, she was gone.

The sun had already been up for hours when the eight men rode out of town on their way to Fort Brown. It would be a ride of almost two weeks, and everyone was most anxious to get started. It was the kind of excitement felt before an adventure had begun, before the hardships of reality had set in.

The sting of Rachel's words was still felt in Heck's mind and on his heart as the group put San Antonio far behind them. He didn't understand women; why couldn't Rachel see he had no choice?

"She had no call to act so harshly toward me. I'm only doing my duty, doing what the good folks of Texas pay me to do," Heck thought. "What gave her the right to only think of herself when it was me who is putting his life in danger to keep the territory safe, and to make sure that folks like her parents can run their businesses without fear of harm. If she wants to go off with that moron Willard, then she could darn well have him. What does it matter to me what she does?"

It wasn't long before he was good and mad at the thought of how she had acted, and this combined with the peacefulness of his surroundings made his spirits change for the better. It was a beautiful day and he was sitting on his favorite horse in the wide-open spaces that he loved. What more could a man ask for?

Riding up next to him, Tommy interrupted his thoughts. "Heck, do you know what you're gonna do when we get back?" He asked.

"What do ya mean, kid?" Heck said, although he had a good idea of what they young man was getting at.

Tommy looked more than a little puzzled that Heck didn't realize what he meant, but he explained it anyway. "I mean do you intend to join the Confederates or stay with the Rangers. Bob told me that we would all be given a choice once we made it back. He said the Captain was gonna lead a new company of Rangers and I could join them if I had a mind to. So, I was just wondering what you were gonna do."

Heck thought for a second and said, "I don't know what I'm gonna do yet kid. It's a big decision and I guess I figured I'd use the time we're gone to make up my mind. What'd ya think you'll do?"

"Well," Tommy said happily, "I guess I'll do what you do. I mean, you've helped me, and I figured I'd stay with you till I helped you out some."

"Is that right?" Heck said smiling. "What makes you think I want you tagging along with me, anyhow?"

With a serious expression, Tommy said, "Well, it's a free country and I reckon if I want to go with you that's my business and not yours." Spurring his horse slightly, he trotted to catch up with Bob and Jim.

The Rangers had taken Tommy in when his family's wagon had been attacked by Juan Cortina's army. He had seen his mother, father, and little sister butchered, and it had taken several months before he even spoke. When he did start speaking, it was only to Heck and Old Tom. Since the morning Old Tom had not woken up, it was Heck that he looked to as a role model. Heck felt a close kinship with Tommy since they were both more or less alone in the world, and both had come to the Rangers when they had nowhere else to go. Tommy had worked in the livery, under the tutelage of Old Tom just as Heck had, and since the old man's death, he had managed the job himself. He had run the livery just like Old Tom had taught him and Heck couldn't have been prouder. He was unsure whether the boy was ready for what they might face on this mission, but Heck was glad he would be with him, and he would do everything possible to protect him.

Heck enjoyed teasing Tommy, much like he would have a little brother. Jefferson had enjoyed teasing him when they were younger, but that was a long time ago, and Heck didn't like spending too much time thinking about it. The brothers had seen each other a few times in the last several years, but mostly just by chance. One of the few planned meetings they had was when Jefferson came to San Antone to tell Heck their father had passed. Heck had spent the night at the ranch after the funeral, but only stayed one night and left early the next morning, without saying anything to his brother. He loved Jefferson and he was sure that Jefferson loved him, but they just didn't have anything tying them together anymore, and they had very little to say that the other wanted to hear. Heck now considered his fellow Rangers his family, and he would do anything for them. The thought of leaving them to fight in the war weighed heavy on his mind as he rode toward Fort Brown.

CHAPTER TWENTY-TWO

Fort Brown sat on a small, sandy rise overlooking the town of Brownsville, and it was little more than a few tents with an old, dilapidated, wooden structure in the center. This structure was the fort's armory, and was the only reason the handful of soldiers still occupied this forsaken position. Outside the decaying walls, the garrison was surrounded on three sides by earthen works, which provided the extent of the redoubt's perimeter fortifications.

The fort had been established as the United States' southernmost defense against an attack by Mexico. Like most outposts on the frontier, it was easily forgotten by the army and War Department. The post offered little opportunity for notoriety or chance of advancement for the officers stationed there. The soldiers were allowed to fall into disrepair, much as the structure in which they served, and were given to drunkenness and all other manner of vice.

The soldiers spent the majority of their time, both on duty as well as off, drinking in the saloons of Brownsville. It was said by the good citizens of that town that they would welcome an invasion by Mexico if they would start by removing the scourge of Fort Brown. When the order came from General Robert Twiggs for all but a small detachment of men to evacuate the post, it was met with great enthusiasm from the community as well as those stationed there.

Lieutenant Sutter and five soldiers remained at the fort after the evacuation to oversee the surrender, and most importantly, to guard the arms that were left. According to the envoy sent by General Twiggs, the Confederates would send a small detachment within a few days to take control of the garrison and her armaments.

Lieutenant Sutter was the junior officer at the post, and as such, it fell to him to surrender the garrison. No ranking officer would accept such a humiliating charge, especially since it would likely mean the end of their career. General Twiggs was the Southern sympathizer and the commanding general, but the army would remember that it was Lieutenant Patrick Sutter who turned over Fort Brown to the enemy. He had been chosen as the sacrificial lamb, and to say he was unhappy about it would be an understatement.

"Lieutenant. Five riders are approaching from the south," Corporal Milburn Anderson said. "They will be here in about an hour. Should the men and I start making the preparations?"

Lieutenant Sutter stood up behind his desk. With a look of relief mixed with annoyance he said, "Yes, please finish the arrangements and then assemble the men on the grounds. I want to get the formalities over with quickly and shake the stink of this place off my feet as soon as possible."

"Yes, sir," the Corporal said. Turning to leave the tent, he stopped and turned back to face the Lieutenant. "Sir, pardon me for saying so, but it's my opinion that the army is giving you a raw deal here. General Twiggs is the turncoat, but they're sacrificing you so they can save their own careers."

The Lieutenant smiled, "Thank you, Corporal, but there is a lot more at stake right now besides my career. The army will likely be fighting a war against these Confederate dogs, and the senior officers will be needed. We must all serve where we can do the most good, and it appears this is the part that I have been chosen to play."

"Don't worry, sir," the Corporal said, "like you said, war is coming and the army will need good officers like yourself. They can't afford to get rid of you that easily."

The Lieutenant knew that Corporal Anderson meant well, but at this moment, he longed to return to his home in Indiana and the relative peacefulness of his father's law practice. He thought army life would be exciting; that he might see the world that he had only read about in the dusty books of his father's library. The world he found was one of boredom and monotony. Army life was a predictable routine, moving from one remote outpost to another, and surrounded by officers who thought of little other than furthering their own careers. Dreaming of his return to Indianapolis society, to civility, and intelligent conversation was the only thing that kept him going.

"Lieutenant, five men approaching the gate, sir," called out a private stationed up in the parapet. "They are not in uniform, and are not carrying any colors."

Sutter thought at least the South would try to put together an outfitted detachment, but he wasn't much surprised. Most of what he'd seen of the South had led him to believe they were more given to bluster and bragging than in military protocol. "Thank you, Private. I wouldn't have expected anything less from this rabble. Let's get this over with. Go ahead and open the gate."

"Yes, sir," the Private said, giving the signal for the gate to be opened.

The whole contingent of Fort Brown stood at attention, in full uniform, as the riders passed through the large wooden gate. Like the Lieutenant, the soldiers were ready to have this humiliation over with so they could hit the trail and get back to the North. Most knew war was coming, and they were anxious to have it begin so they could repay these Confederates on the battle field.

Lieutenant Sutter and Corporal Anderson approached the men on horseback, ready to do what had to be done. Looking at the group of riders, however, Sutter immediately recognized he had made a terrible mistake. These men were not military, not even by Southern standards. They were unkempt, filthy, and armed to the teeth. His heart sank as he noticed that most of the detachment were Mexican and their guns were not in their holsters. "What is going on here?" he said, unable to believe what he was seeing.

The lead rider smiled and said, "This was even easier than Senor Cortina said it would be. Thank you." Without saying another word, the man raised his pistol and fired two quick shots, hitting both Lieutenant Sutter and Corporal Anderson between the eyes.

The stunned Private up in the parapet could not believe what he was seeing, and swiftly pulled his rifle up to his shoulder to fire. His finger had almost reached the trigger when a rifle shot from somewhere in the distance struck him in the back. His lifeless body fell forward and off the parapet to the hard earth fifteen feet below.

"My compadres, my name is Victor Ruiz and as you can see there has been a change in command," the man said in mock laughter, gesturing towards the lifeless bodies of the Lieutenant and Corporal. "We are here on behalf of Senor Juan Cortina. We do not wish to take up much of your time, so I only have one question." Walking his horse up to a disheveled old private, he stopped a few feet away and smiled. "Can I have your name, amigo?"

The private was visibly shaken by what he had just witnessed and felt like he would vomit. "Uh. Uh. My name is Davis Janner," he stammered.

"Well Senor Janner," Victor said, "I have only one question for you. The weapons that have been crated up for transport. Please to tell me where I might find them."

Davis was a lousy soldier and had spent most of his ten years in the cavalry either in the stockade or drunk. He had only stayed in the army to keep from winding up in jail, and he certainly felt no loyalty to the United States government, but he did have respect for Lieutenant Sutter. The Lieutenant had stood up for him once when he had been drunk on duty and allowed him to remain on post rather than being sent to hard labor at the military prison. Davis would be damned if he was going to tell his killer anything. "I don't know where the guns are. I'm just a lowly private, the officers don't tell me nothing."

Victor's smile quickly faded from his face. "That's too bad Senor. Flaco," he said to the man directly behind him, and then made a slashing motion across his throat with his hand.

The man called Flaco raised his shotgun and fired. The blast struck Davis in his midsection, knocking him backwards almost two feet. The private was dead before his body hit the ground.

Riding up to the next soldier in formation, Victor repeated his question. "Please senor, tell me what I want to know. We only want the guns. Nobody else has to die today."

"The small arms are in crates in the building behind you. The cannons are in the large tent over yonder," the young soldier said, gesturing to a canvas covered structure.

The smile returned to Victor's face. In his most jovial tone he said, "Thank you, amigo. That is all we wanted. You are all free to go." Turning his horse around he trotted behind his men and whispered an order.

The four men lined up in front of the remaining soldiers and opened fire. They each emptied their pistols into the helpless men, and made sure that each one was dead before riding away.

Victor continued to smile while surveying the scene. Juan Cortina was a man who rewarded success lavishly, and Victor could only imagine what his would be for taking care of this matter with such ease.

"Buenos amigos!" Victor yelled to the men. "Carlos, you and Mateo go over to that tent and load up the crates. The rest of us will make the cannons ready to transport. Hurry up. Once we're finished, there will be tequila and senoritas for everyone in Matamoras."

CHAPTER TWENTY-THREE

The lone rider ambled along the half lit, mostly deserted street. Preparing for the day, the town's few shopkeepers were busy sweeping the new layers of dust back into the street. A blazing sun was just beginning to crest over the eastern horizon, offering a hint of the scorching heat to come. The white adobe facade of the Spanish mission stood as a silent guardian over the town of Brownsville. Nestled along the banks of the Rio Grande River, and less than a half day's ride north of Matamoras, Mexico, Brownsville was a small town populated mostly by small ranchers. It was a harsh place to live and required hard people to pull a living from her soil. The summers were brutally hot and dry, and the winters could freeze a man right down to the bone. Winds would blow up from

Mexico, capable of ripping the hide off a cow. Rainfall each year amounted to only five to six inches, and it usually came all at once. It would wash away crops, topsoil, and houses.

Javier Lopez rode slowly, looking at each building carefully as he passed by. Finding the one he was looking for, he swung his good leg over the saddle horn and eased himself down to the street below. Lopez double checked the sign to be sure he had the right building. It read "Cameron County Sheriff's Office." Slowly he limped up to the small door and stepped inside.

He had been the guest in many sheriff's offices, and every one was the same. The same shabby desk. The same smell of coffee. The same row of cells in the back, reeking with the smell of human waste.

Behind the desk was a fat slob of a sheriff, maybe in his mid-thirties, dressed in a dirty shirt, covered by a moth eaten brown vest. He was working on a plate of eggs and bacon, washing it down with a cup of the aforementioned coffee.

"Something I can do for ya, stranger?" The sheriff said, between mouthfuls of eggs.

"Si senor. I have information about Juan Cortina," Lopez said.

Putting down his fork, the sheriff leaned closer, as if trying to get a better look at the man interrupting his breakfast.

"Mister," he said, "if you know something about Cortina, you'd better just tell me."

Lopez set down in the chair opposite the sheriff and said, "Cortina and his men are camped not far from here. I can take you and your men there. There's still a reward for him, right?"

The sheriff nodded, "There is a reward, but I don't have any men, and I'm sure as hell not going after him with just you."

"I see," said Lopez, with the start of a smile forming at the corners of his mouth. With a surprisingly quick motion, given the man's advanced age, Lopez grabbed the sheriff's head and slammed his face into the wooden desk top. The sheriff's nose broke immediately upon making contact with the hard desk. He thrashed about wildly, sending the remnants of his breakfast flying across the room. Lifting the big man's head with his right hand, Lopez took his knife from its scabbard with his left and cut the sheriff's throat.

After dragging his body to the far corner of the room, Javier took his place behind the desk. He propped his stiff leg up on the desk and rubbed it slowly. His leg hurt the worst in the mornings, especially when he had spent days in the saddle.

The leg was a "gift" from the Comanche who captured him up along the plains some twenty years earlier. The warrior spent days torturing him with a lance and a red-hot poker. He used the poker to repeatedly burn him, and his leg had been burned all the way down to the bone.

Lopez had been part of a gang of slavers who had raided a Comanche village. The gang had murdered all of the warriors and captured most of women and children, who were taken below the border to be sold as slaves. Lopez admired the Comanche as brutal warriors who showed no mercy to their enemies. Personally, he couldn't help admire the warrior who crippled him, but that didn't stop him from crushing the man's skull with a rock in order to make his escape.

CHAPTER TWENTY-FOUR

Juan Cortina was a tall man who rode high in the saddle. He dressed in the traditional black breeches and waistcoat of a Mexican Vaquero. He wore his large sombrero pulled low, obscuring his facial features. A bushy beard seemed to form his mouth into a perpetual scowl. He cut a most impressive figure riding his black Arabian, and those he passed couldn't help but stare at him out of the corner of their eye. They would do so with extreme care, so as not to be noticed. Cortina's cruelty to those who offended him was known far and wide. The fear he inspired preceded him, but was even more keenly felt after he was gone.

Cortina rode into Brownsville followed by six of his killers. They thundered through town, stirring up a cloud of dust, which served to further enhance the fear of the townspeople. Those on the streets quickly abandoned whatever tasks they were occupied with, seeking the imagined safety of whatever structure was close at hand. Stopping in front of the general store the men dismounted, surveying their surroundings against the unlikely event that someone would be foolish enough to challenge them.

"Manuel," Cortina said, "you and Jorge get the supplies we need and then meet us down at the cantina." Manuel and Jorge were useless and the sight of them made Cortina angry, but they were usually competent enough to handle such rudimentary tasks as fetching supplies.

"Si jefe," Manuel said.

"C'mon amigos," their leader said in a more cheerful tone, "let's eat before we head back home."

Manuel and Jorge entered the dry goods store as if they were walking into their own home. The proprietor and his wife watched nervously as the two men began grabbing items off the shelves.

"Five-pound bag of flour, two bags of coffee, one bag of sugar," Manuel said. "No wait, we'd better make that two bags. The boys like Cerra's sweet bread. Just start stacking it by the door."

Eyeing the owner, Manuel walked over and demanded, "I need ten bags of forty-four caliber shot and five bags of powder."

Sheepishly the man turned to comply, but caught the expression on his wife's face and froze in his tracks. Turning back to Manuel the little man said, "Mister, you are getting a lot of things, and I'm going to need to see your money. We are happy to sell you merchandise, but I need to make sure you can pay."

Manuel stared at the man and his wife coolly. Jorge stopped stacking the supplies and joined his friend. "Amigo," Manuel said, "we work for Juan Cortina. Do you believe Senor Cortina is a thief? Are you saying we would steal?"

The shopkeeper shook his head and said, "No mister. I do not believe you are a thief."

"Good," he said putting his hand on the man's shoulder. "Now I want you to apologize for insulting El Jefe. He is a very proud man and would not want his reputation tarnished by some worthless shopkeeper."

The store owner remained silent for some time, cutting his eyes towards his wife. She said nothing, but he felt her disgust at his cowardice just the same. Steeling his resolve, he looked the outlaw in the eye and said, "No. I will not apologize. You are all thieves and murderers. The law will catch up with you one day."

Manuel and Jorge both started laughing wildly. "Look Jorge," he said, "the sheep has become the coyote. I like this little man. He makes me laugh." Turning back to the couple he said, "You are very brave, and you may be right. We might all die at the end of a noose one day, but today is not that day." With that he drew his pistol, killing the man and his wife.

Hearing the gunshots from down the street, Cortina opened a bottle of tequila and poured a drink for each of his men. "Ah, amigos," he yelled, so that the whole cantina could hear, "it appears that Manuel and Jorge have finished gathering the supplies."

Taking the cue from their leader, everyone began laughing. The only one not laughing was Zapata, Cortina's right hand man and favorite killer. Zapata never laughed, or smiled for that matter. He never seemed to take pleasure in anything. He was a cold-blooded killer, but he didn't even find enjoyment in that. Cortina was his boss and the closest thing he had to a friend, so when he wanted him to kill, Zapata did so without question.

Even the worst men feared Zapata, but not just because he was a vicious murderer, but because he often killed in the most horrific and gruesome manner in order to make a point. It was said that the closest thing to pleasure for Zapata was inventing new and horrible ways to inflict pain on the enemies of Juan Cortina.

Turning his attention to three men eating breakfast at a table in the corner, Cortina said, "Amigos, are you the gentlemen who own those fine horses out front?"

The oldest of the three men spoke up, "Yes, those are our horses."

Cortina walked over to their table and sat down. Downing his shot of tequila, he said, "They are indeed beautiful animals. How much will you take for them?"

The older man thought for a moment before replying, "Mister, we don't want any trouble. I own a small farm and these men work for me. These are our only horses and they are not for sale."

Cortina motioned for one of his men to pour him another drink. After taking a sip he asked, "What is your name senor?"

"I'm Louis Walker," he replied.

Cortina extended his hand to the farmer. "Very nice to meet you, Senor Walker. My name is Juan Cortina and I own a small ranch just south of the border." Louis Walker carefully reached out and shook the man's hand. "Those really are magnificent animals," Cortina said. "I've always believed that Texas horses are much inferior compared to those bred in Mexico, so that makes me think that maybe you stole them. Is that correct, senor? Did you steal those horses? You see amigo, as a rancher I have very little patience for horse thieves, and I usually deal with them in a most harsh manner.

"We're not horse thieves, mister. Those horses are ours and we intend to breed and sell a whole lot more just like 'em."

Finishing his drink, Cortina turned the glass upside down on the table. "I tell you what senor, we will take those horses back to Mexico and let you off with just a warning this time."

"Like hell you will," Walker shouted. "You ain't taking our horses."

Juan Cortina shrugged his shoulders and stood up. "I tried to give you the chance to atone for your crime senor, but apparently, you do not care to. Therefore, you will have to be punished." He shot a glance to Zapata and pointed towards Walker with his thumb. Without a second of hesitation, Zapata lowered his shotgun and pulled the trigger. The blast hit the rancher in the back, causing his body to crash through the table and onto the floor.

Walker's men both stared in disbelief at the blood-stained body of their boss, as fear griped their throats, rendering them unable to vocalize the anger they felt at the senseless murder.

Cortina signaled for the two men to be taken outside, and then turned to address one of his men. "Guillermo."

"Si jefe?" The man replied.

"Show these two how we deal with horse thieves in Mexico," Cortina said.

Guillermo was by far the largest member of Cortina's army. He stood more than six and a half feet and weighed more than two hundred and fifty pounds. More prominent than his girth, was the scar that ran across his face, from his right ear to his chin. He moved slowly, but was stronger than any three men combined, and if he got his big hands around someone's neck it would all be over for them except for the burial. Guillermo was fair with a gun, but his hands had dealt far more death than his pistol.

Guillermo chose the tallest of the men's horses, a roan mustang standing over sixteen hands. Lifting his considerable frame into the saddle, he removed the rope hanging on the side, wrapping one end around the saddle horn.

Cortina put his arms around the young ranchers and asked, "Amigos. Which one of you is the oldest?"

The man on his right said, "I am. I'm twenty-six and Hershel here is twenty-two."

Cortina patted him on the back, and removed his arm from Hershel. "I see, and what is your name?"

"I'm Billy. Look mister, take our horses. We worked for Mister Walker, but we don't want to die for him."

"You think we want to steal your horses? No. No, senor. We are not her to steal, but to punish those that would take from us." Pushing the young man into the street, Cortina said, "Ok Guillermo, take care of this thief."

Guillermo threw the other end of his rope around Billy's neck and spurred his horse to a gallop, dragging the young man behind him.

Cortina put his pistol to the other man's head and said, "Hershel, the one thing I hate more than a thief is a coward." The bullet tore through the man's head, and covered Cortina in his blood.

Leaving the young rancher's body in the street, Cortina turned to his men and said, "Manuel, did you and Jorge get the supplies loaded?"

"Si, jefe," the man replied.

"Good," Cortina said, "let's saddle up. Victor and the others should be finished at the fort by now and we will all ride for home. Zapata, please go to the Sheriff's office and tell Javier we are leaving."

A few miles outside of town, Cortina rendezvoused with Victor and the rest of the men from the fort. "Ah, Victor! You have had a fruitful day, I see. These guns will give us the power to take whatever we want. Let's ride for home now."

"Thank you, Patron," Victor said, "but there is something you should know. There is a detachment of soldiers on the way here to retrieve these guns. The men at the fort thought we were them, so they could be here at any time."

Cortina pulled at the end of his mustache, as was his habit when thinking. "I see. I don't care to spend the next several days looking over my shoulder. Victor, take Manuel and Jorge and cut their trail. I want you to find them and get rid of them."

Without hesitation, Victor said, "Si Patron, we go at once."

"Thank you, amigo," Cortina said with a smile, "We will wait a few days in Matamoras for you to catch up."

CHAPTER TWENTY-FIVE

The Rangers and soldiers had been on the trail for over a week and a half, with almost no sleep. They were all anxious to finish their mission, so it was decided they would keep on the move as much as possible, figuring they could rest a few days once they reached Brownsville.

The soldiers and Rangers had only spoken a few words to each other since leaving San Antonio. Each group had their own opinions about the direction the national winds were blowing, and they had very little respect or interest in what the other group had to say.

The soldiers were anxious to take up arms against a government they felt was destroying their way of life. All four men were from Missouri and were convinced that the government was actively encouraging the abolitionist forces in Kansas to make raids across the border. The Jayhawkers from Kansas were nothing more than pillagers and murderers, who justified their horrible acts through their desire to end slavery. What the four young men failed to take into account was that the Missouri Border Ruffians were crossing the state lines and committing equally deplorable acts on the innocent civilians in Kansas. The fact that their way of life included keeping fellow human beings in bondage also seemed to be conveniently forgotten by the young soldiers.

For their part, the Rangers had very little knowledge or interest in politics, and even less interest in protecting the way of life of a bunch of lazy plantation owners who forced others to do the work that made them rich. Like most Texans, they felt a world apart from the rest of the country. In many ways, they still thought of Texas as its own country, and preferred to handle their own affairs instead of relying on help from Washington. The US Army had set up forts in Texas and worked with the Rangers to fight the hostile Comanche, so in this regard, the four Rangers had warm feelings toward those that the Confederates wished to face on the battlefield.

The group rode in formation, with the Rangers always in the lead, and they were making about thirty miles a day. When not in the saddle, the two groups stayed separate, with each making their own camp, and cooking their own meals. Heck had tried to tell the four green soldiers that they should not make camp so far away from them, but his advice was met with such contempt that he refused to try and reason with them any further. "They're darned fools and don't care to listen to good sense," Heck said.

Bob just laughed. "Don't waste your time. Those boys are so passionate about the cause that they don't trust anyone who don't figure the same way."

The Rangers picked a spot along the bank of the Frio River to make their camp. They spread their bedrolls under a rocky outcropping that formed a shallow cavern. It not only offered shelter, but also served to protect their campfire. The river was barely a trickle here, but was sufficient to water both men and horses, although due to its heavy alkaline taste, it was the source of much complaining.

The soldiers chose a spot about fifteen yards downstream to make their camp. It was a poor choice for a camp. The Rangers tried to dissuade them, but of course the more they tried to convince them, the more entrenched the soldiers became in their position. Their camp was out in the open, on top of the river bank, and offered no refuge from the elements or from attack. The soldiers were unaccustomed to the necessity of concealing themselves, and had built their campfire too large. Anyone who was looking would be able to see it from miles away.

The four Rangers sat around their campfire finishing the last few drops of coffee in their cups. The water tasted horrible by itself, but made a good, strong pot of mud. They had been on the trail for almost two weeks and not a word of the coming storm had been uttered. Each of them recognized that war was almost a certainty, and would rip the nation apart. They were only simple lawmen, but they understood that the conflict coming would be a bloody, bitter fight, and no man, woman, or child would escape its affects.

"So, what are you boys gonna do when we get back?" Heck asked.

Bob stoked the fire, causing it to roar back to life. "I reckon I'll stay with the Rangers," he said. "The Captain will be needin' every man he can get. If we don't stay, Texas will fall back into the hands of the bandits and Comanche. Mexico might even try to come back and take over."

Heck wasn't so sure. "Captain McCullough said that the abolitionists were planning to invade Texas. Wouldn't it make better sense to stop them up North before they can make it down here?" He said.

"Captain McCullough is itchin' for a fight and would say anything to push Texas into this war," Jim said, carefully scanning the perimeter one more time before turning in. "He's got political aspirations and figures glory in battle is the fastest route to a place in the new government."

"What about you, Heck?" Tommy asked. "What are you gonna do?"

Heck stretched out on his blanket. "I don't know, kid. I reckon I'll cross that bridge when I get to it. You'd better turn in. I have a feelin' we got a long trail ahead of us." Pulling his Colt from its holster, he laid it beside him underneath his blanket. Since the Rangers had driven out the Comanche, Heck found it much easier to sleep on the trail, but he still fell asleep quicker with his hands wrapped around the walnut grips of his pistol.

In their camp, the new Confederate soldiers were wrapped up in their own bedrolls. They each felt as if they were taking their first steps on a grand adventure. All were certain of just one thing, that they would be part of history. The would be present at the birth of a new and great nation. The boredom of farm life and the tedious existence of a shop keeper were far behind them.

"What do you think of the Rangers?" Mathias asked, to no one in particular. He was not yet ready to fall asleep, and was curious what his companions thought of their guides.

"They're no better than cowboys," Daniel said. "I've seen a few of them in town, and they care more about drinkin' and carousing than they do about keeping the peace. These Texians are a rough bunch and we sure don't need them to whoop the Yankees."

Mathias shook his head with utter disdain and contempt. "They care nothing about honor and the glory of our cause," he said. "They are more interested in hard drink and dirty women than in fighting for their homes. We don't need their kind and it would be just as well with me if Jefferson Davis gave this land back to Mexico and the savages with it."

Clel spoke up in an effort to bring reason to the conversation. "Our homes may at this moment be threatened by those murdering Jayhawkers. We need men and arms to beat back those devils, and General McCullough and the Texas Rangers are going to help us get them. I don't care how these Texians choose to live their lives. I will show them respect for what they are doing for us, and as for their numerous shortcomings, we should follow the example of Jesus and help them through prayer and forgiveness."

Cotton didn't know much about the issues involved in the present crisis. It was expected by his father that as the oldest son he should do his part in the Southern struggle. "My Pa said that the Jayhawkers is gonna get the Negroes stirred up and they will murder all the White folk in their sleep. He paid the money to outfit me to whoop those that would try to kill us, and he told me it would be better if I died for a just cause than to let Lincoln's Army set one foot on Missouri soil. If they're willing to die alongside me, I reckon I can forgive their sinful ways."

"Well, let's hope we can beat the Yankees and still make it back to our homes and families," Clel said with a yawn. "We better turn in. Those Rangers are gonna push hard tomorrow and I'm not gonna have them look on us Missourians as a bunch of slackers."

"Jim. Jim," Heck said, "Wake up. Something's moving over there at the soldier's camp."

Stirring slowly, Jim opened his eyes. "What?" he said. "What are you talking about?"

"There's something moving over at the soldier's camp," he said.

"What's going on?" Bob said, climbing out of his bedroll.

"Sshh," Heck said, "I think we're under attack." He pointed in the direction of the other camp, and they all could vaguely make out several dark shapes moving in the distance.

Clel woke to the sound of shuffling footsteps approaching from the river bank. Jumping up, he glanced all around him, rubbing the sleep from his eyes, and strained against the darkness. "Who's out there? Daniel, Mathias," he said. "Something's out—"

His words stuck in his throat. A burning pain consumed his whole body. He tried to turn around, but could not move. Dropping to his knees he reached behind him and felt the steel of a knife in his back. Clel tried to get back to his feet, but the burning pain was being replaced by a numbness that left him weak and unable to focus his thoughts. Fighting against the numbness, he slowly turned his head towards the sound of scuffling behind him. He saw the blurry image of someone standing over Daniel and Cotton, repeatedly hacking away at them with a large sickle shaped blade. Clel used his fingertips and feet to drag himself over to his friends, but the darkness was beginning to consume him, and after only a few inches he was engulfed by the veil of complete silence.

Manuel wiped the blood from his blade while Jorge started gathering the dead men's belongings.

"These soldiers are poorer than the peasants in my village. There's nothing here that is worth the effort to carry back to the horses," Jorge said, as he tossed their meager possessions aside.

"Hold it right there! We're Texas Rangers. Drop your weapons before we start shooting," Jim said, stepping out of the tall grass. Manuel turned around to face Jim, while Jorge reached for his pistol. He was sure that he could kill the Ranger before he was able to shoot them both.

"You pull that gun and you're dead where you stand, friend," Heck said from the shadows. He had learned from experience that when apprehending bandits, it was always best to go at them from different directions.

After disarming the bandits, they tied their hands and feet and laid them on their stomachs. Jim and Heck examined the soldiers, but it was too late. They were all dead.

"Both these men are dead." Heck said. "I can't tell which ones they are. That butcher went at both of 'em pretty hard."

Jim looked at the other body and said, "This one is Clel, one of the farm boys. There are only two bodies over there?"

"Yeah," Heck said. "They might have taken the other one into the brush and killed him." Heck searched around as best he could in the dark, but didn't see anything.

A rustling in the grass drew both men's attention. The sound was coming from no more than ten feet away, but it was too dark to see anything. Heck looked at Jim, who signaled for him to check it out while he covered the two prisoners.

Heck crouched down and made his way towards the noise. The rustling was coming closer and Heck laid as flat as he could make himself. In the dark, he figured it would be difficult for anyone to see him, and he would be able to shoot before they did.

Footsteps could now be heard as well as the rustling, and Heck could make out a silhouette only a few feet away. He knew he should go ahead and fire, as there was enough of a target for a reasonably sure kill, but Heck never liked to fire without being perfectly sure what he was shooting at. The figure came out of the brush as Heck took aim and prepared to fire.

"Heck wait. It's Mathias," Jim said.

Heck kept his gun on him, while he carefully examined the man. The dark figure came into focus as the black shape gave way to the recognizable form of the young soldier. "What were you doing out there? Do you realize I almost shot you?" Heck said, more than a little annoyed that he had almost shot the young man.

"I uh. I was hiding over there," the young man stammered nervously. "I had gone to the privy and when I came back I heard what was happening, so I hid out in the grass until I was sure you had 'em." He suddenly realized how cowardly he sounded and said, "I left my gun in camp. There was nothing I could do." Walking slowly into camp he sheepishly looked over at the blood-soaked bodies. "They're all dead, aren't they?"

"Yeah kid. They're all dead," Jim said, unable or unwilling to hide his disgust.

"What do ya want to do with them?" Heck asked, pointing toward the two murderers.

Jim looked off into the distance and said, "We'll wait for Bob to get back and see if these killers have any friends out there." He knew what would have to be done, but didn't want to say it out loud yet.

"So, are you boys with Cortina's group?" Jim said, to the two men lying on the ground. Jim knew they were. Juan Cortina controlled the largest band of outlaws in northeastern Mexico, and no one raided into this part of Texas unless they worked for him.

"I don't know who you're talking about, senor," Manuel said with a sly smile. "My friend and I work alone."

"Heck. Jim. It's me, Bob. I'm coming in alone," Bob yelled from the river bank, not wanting to risk getting shot by his own men. After identifying himself, he made his way up the bank and into camp.

"Did you see anything out there?" Jim said.

Bob nodded. "Yeah. I tracked one to the other side of the river, but he lit out fast. His horse was hidden over there in the brush and he rode off to the southeast."

"You can bet he'll be hightailing it back to Cortina to tell him we're still alive," Jim said. He wished they could chase after him, but in the dark, it would be suicide.

"Are all the soldier's dead?" Bob asked, not seeing Mathias sitting in the darkness.

"No," Heck replied. "The kid here had to drain it, so he was over yonder when they were attacked. He hid out in the tall grass until it was all over."

Bob felt guilty about it, but he couldn't help chuckling a little. "Well, that was one lucky piss, although I probably wouldn't tell that story too much if I were you." He looked around the camp, shaking his head in disgust. "What a mess," he said. "This mission's gone from bad to worse in a big hurry. Let's bury our dead and get back on the trail. I have a feeling we need to double time it to the fort. The men there were the only ones who knew we would be headed that way, so that means that Cortina has already been there."

The Rangers took turns burying the three soldiers, while the others guarded the prisoners. They hit solid rock a few feet down, making it impossible to dig any further. The dead would have to accept spending eternity in a shallow grave, a decision Mathias said the others would understand given the circumstances. Heck believed the graves would suffice to keep the animals from getting at them, but the first heavy rain would surely wash away the soil and expose those contained within.

After burial and a short service, the group turned to the two prisoners and debated their fate.

"We need to ride hard for Fort Brown," Bob said. "If we push hard we can make it in a little more than a day, but there's no way we could do that while guarding two prisoners. Ordinarily, I'd say we'd just deal with 'em ourselves, but they killed three soldiers, which makes it a job for the Army."

"We don't know what's waiting for us at the fort, and Mathias here is the only other soldier for at least three hundred miles. I sure don't plan on dragging them back to San Antone," Heck argued.

Jim rubbed his chin, trying to get used to his new whiskers. Rubbing his chin was his preferred method of solving a problem, but the wiry beard seemed to be interfering with the process. He usually liked to shave on extended campaigns, but he had forgotten his razor back in town. After a moment, he thought he had hit on a solution to the present problem. "Why don't we let Private Mathias decide what to do with 'em. Like you said, he is the only Army representative we have and I figure he's at least smart enough to settle the fate of these varmints. Since he's also a witness to the crime, it should really shorten the length of the trial." Jim gave the young soldier a smile and a friendly clap on the back.

Mathias looked over at the prisoners, who were still lying on their stomachs. The men they had killed were friends of his as well as comrades in arms, and Mathias wanted to see justice done for them. "I pronounce them guilty of murder," he said loudly. "What do we do with 'em now?"

Bob thought about what should be done, and then answered. "The penalty for murder is death. We'll have to kill them."

"Are we really prepared to kill these men?" Jim asked. He didn't have a problem killing butchers like these, but he didn't want any of them to get into trouble with the law. Judge Williams liked to have live prisoners to try and sentence, and had no patience for those that tried to go around the legal process.

Heck and Bob pulled both prisoners to their feet and walked them over to the tall grass where they were ordered to stand. The sun was just beginning to crest over the horizon, illuminating the area, and for the first time, revealed the evidence of what had taken place only a few hours before.

Bob spoke to everyone just out of ear shot of those about to be executed. "We will each fire two shots at the condemned men, and afterwards I will check to make sure they are both dead. Are we all in agreement?"

All four nodded in agreement. Bob handed Mathias the extra pistol that he kept in his boot. "Have you ever killed anyone?" Bob said.

"No I have not. I have never killed anything." Mathias answered unashamed.

Bob smiled at him and said, "Well, these murdering rascals are good ones to start with. When we're ready, just pull the hammer back and fire. You'll need to take aim again after the first shot because it will kick just a little." Walking over to the condemned prisoners he told them, "You both have been found guilty of murder and have been sentenced to death. Do you have anything to say before we get on with it?"

Manuel spit at him and said, "You can't kill us. You're not a judge. Juan Cortina will kill you all. You will all die, just like all those gringos at your fort."

"What are you talking about?" Jim said. Stepping forward he pressed the barrel of his pistol to Manuel's head. "What happened at the fort? You'd better start talking right now."

Manuel seemed amused at the Ranger's anger. "What are you going to do, senor?" He said. "You kill us twice? It makes no difference now. The guns are all gone and the soldiers are all dead, just like you all will be before long."

Jim walked over to Jorge and put the gun to his head, and said, "What about you, amigo? Do you feel like talking?"

"It's no use, senor," Manuel said, "he doesn't speak English.

Lowering his weapon, Jim said, "We need to hurry. If he's telling the truth, Cortina will be heading back across the border with those guns."

"Tommy," Bob said, "get the horses saddled and ready to ride while we take care of this business. Jim's right, we need to ride hard."

Tommy walked down to the river where the horses were tied. He didn't fully understand what was happening, but one thing was clear, it seemed he would get his chance to see justice done for his parents. His time with the Rangers was finally paying off, he thought, as a smile of satisfaction spread across his face.

"May God have mercy on your souls," Bob said to the condemned. He then joined the others standing a few feet away. "Gentlemen, ready your arms. Take aim. Fire!"

All four men fired their guns. The prisoners' bodies jerked from the shots and then fell to the ground. Bob walked over and examined the bodies carefully, pronouncing both dead.

CHAPTER TWENTY-SIX

Victor was used to a life of hardship, so riding for two days without stopping didn't seem like much of a feat. He wanted to reach Cortina as soon as possible to tell him that there would soon be three Texas Rangers on their trail. Arriving in Matamoros, he immediately rode to the Hotel Espinoza where Cortina occupied the whole third floor when in town.

The Hotel Espinoza was a dilapidated building made of adobe and wood, and served as a base of operations for Cortina when the gang made raids into Texas. The hotels patrons consisted mainly of transient outlaws who were hiding out in Matamoros for one reason or another. Regardless of who happened to be staying there, when Juan

Cortina showed up, everyone occupying the third floor were immediately relocated.

Walking into the hotel, Victor walked past the three sentries posted in the lobby and climbed the red carpeted staircase to the third floor. After being allowed to pass by three more guards posted in the hallway, Victor entered Cortina's room.

"Ah, Victor," Cortina said warmly. "I trust you had a successful mission. Are the soldiers taken care of?"

Victor hesitated for a moment, trying to think of the best way to deliver the bad news. Juan Cortina was not one who ever took bad news or failure well. "No, Patron. Three of the soldiers appeared dead, but one is still alive."

"I see," said Cortina. "I wanted all of them dead, Victor, and you're telling me there is one still alive. I can usually count on you to carry out my orders without failing, but you have disappointed me this time. With that being said, it seems our problem could still be removed. If there is only one left, he will probably bury his dead and head back North. I suppose I can forgive this one mistake amigo."

Victor took a deep breath and said, "It's not just that, Jefe. There were three Texas Rangers with them and they captured Manuel and Jorge. I barely got away without being captured."

"Idiot!" Cortina snapped, his face turning red with anger. "It would have been better to leave the soldiers alive and kill the Rangers. Soldiers are weak and useless without someone giving them orders, but Rangers are fierce fighters and they don't give up as easily as soldiers. So, we have lost two men and strengthened the Rangers resolve in the process."

160

"I am sorry Patron," Victor explained. "I will do whatever I can to make up for my mistake."

"Don't worry, amigo. I forgive you," Cortina said. "Manuel and Jorge were useless and they will hardly be missed, but you, Victor, are very important to me. Since you are so very important, I will give you the chance to make up for your mistake. Now please leave me. I must make plans for our friends from Texas."

CHAPTER TWENTY-SEVEN

Pushing their horses past the point of exhaustion, Heck, Jim, Bob, Tommy, and Mathias rode hard through the night. Each man struggled against the urge to close their eyes, as lack of sleep combined with oppressive heat, produced overpowering fatigue. Their only repast consisted of some hard biscuits and a few sips of water consumed in the saddle.

Crossing the Nueces River, the group paused a few hours to water the horses and get a little rest.

"How much further do we have to go?" Heck said. He didn't want to appear anxious, but he knew a fight was coming and didn't like the idea of being overly tired when it came.

"A few more hours, I reckon," Bob said. "We've made our crossing further up river than I'm used to, so I don't really have my bearings yet. You can smell the salt in the air from the Gulf of Mexico, so I know it can't be much further."

Jim shot Heck a knowing look. "You itching for a fight so bad that you can't enjoy a few moments to rest your bones?"

"I ain't itchin' for nothing," Heck said, with a touch of annoyance, "but those rascals got one coming, and it's gonna be us giving it to 'em. I just want to know when to be expecting it, that's all."

"It will suit me just fine if we can accomplish our mission without going to war with Cortina," Bob said. "We're here to retrieve the arms from the fort and get back to San Antone with them as quickly as possible. My hope is to do that without wasting precious time in a fight. We are not going to let a thirst for vengeance lead us away from why we're here."

Heck took a long drink from his canteen, thinking about Bob's words. "There is no way around a fight and you know that better than I do, Bob. It's not about vengeance. He's got the guns and he ain't gonna just let us come and take them back because we have a mission. I know that you think I'm always looking for a scrape, but you're wrong. I would rather avoid trouble, but if it's gotta come, I'd rather it be on my terms."

Bob nodded in agreement. "You may be right kid, but I'm gonna hold out hope that we may avoid it, at least for a while. It will come to a fight at some point, but like you said, I would rather it be on our terms when we are in force, not just four men and a boy. No matter what may come, we must ride hard and get to the fort."

After another few hours ride, the group came up over a little rise and down below they could see the town of Brownsville. To the southwest, the ramparts of Fort Brown could barely be seen, but even at this distance they could tell something was wrong. Looking through his spyglass, Bob saw that indeed there was something very wrong. He could see many people milling around the fort, but none were wearing uniforms.

Bob turned to the rest of the group and said, "There's a problem at the fort. I see many people around it, but they're not soldiers. We'd better move it along."

Arriving at the gates to the fort, the group was hailed by a tall man wearing a tin star. "Hold it right there," the man said. "Who are you and what can I do for you?"

Jim shaded his eyes with his hand in order to get a better look at the man who was speaking to him. "I'm Corporal King and my companions are Corporal Curtis, Corporal Carson, and private uh, well—"

Mathias spoke up and said, "Jones. I'm Private Jones of the Confederate Army, sir, and well, I guess I'm in charge here. Who are you?"

The man scratched his head and said, "I'm Oliver Grayson, temporary Sheriff's Deputy of Cameron County, and I'm guarding the fort until the army shows up. Did you say you're a private and you're in charge?"

Bob, trying to speed things up a bit said, "What he meant was the Confederate Army has taken control of Fort Brown and we're here to secure and transport the arms."

"Well," Oliver said, "you're too late for that. Juan Cortina and his boys took 'em."

"Where are the soldiers that were stationed here? We were told there would be a small detachment here to meet us." Jim said, pretty sure he didn't want to hear the answer.

Oliver looked at the ground, thinking of a way to soften his words, but could think of no way to put a better light on things. "They're all dead. Cortina's men killed every one of them. They also killed the Sheriff and several others in town. Then they loaded up most of the cannon and crates before riding back across the border."

"They are a murdering bunch," Heck said angrily. "You mean they took all the guns?"

Oliver pointed to the tent where the cannons had been stored. "All of 'em except one big artillery piece. The caisson had a busted wheel and they couldn't haul it out."

"What'd ya want to do now, Bob. They've crossed the border and we can't go after 'em, but I don't care to go back and tell the Cap'n that we let Cortina get away with all the guns either," Jim said, pushing his fingers through his hair.

Bob wasn't sure what the answer was, but Jim was right. They had been sent by their new government to secure the arms, and it wouldn't go well with them if they returned empty handed. "I don't know what to do," he said, "but we'd better think of something."

"I tell you what we do, we go after them," Heck said. "Why are we even discussing this?"

Bob put his hand up to calm the young Ranger. "Slow down kid, and think about what you're saying. We have no authority across the border. In fact, the Mexicans could consider it an act of war. If we were to get caught we'd probably be executed or at least left to rot in some prison." Bob hadn't survived hundreds of enemy engagements to die in some prison dungeon for a government that he wasn't even sure he wanted to be a part of. The way he saw it, the Confederacy was controlled by a bunch of rich planters who were willing to tear the country apart in order to keep their supply of free labor.

"You know that other Rangers have crossed the border chasing bandits and they made it back," Heck said. "You can't tell me that you're okay with just letting them get away with murder. We are supposed to protect the people of Texas from scum like Cortina, but he thinks he can come up here and do as he pleases. These killers butchered Tommy's family and how many more to boot. Are you going to tell him that we should just head back home with our tails between our legs? Let's take a vote and see what we all think."

Pushing Jim aside, Bob grabbed Heck by the shirt. He stood an inch or two taller than him, but to Heck it might as well have been two feet. "Listen to me good, kid," Bob said in a tone that Heck took for anger, but was really just frustration. "Executing those murdering skunks back there was one thing, but this is something else and it won't be made by no vote. The Captain put me in charge, so if we go after Cortina it will be my decision only. You've become a good Ranger, kid, but don't question my authority again."

"Okay, let's all just take it easy," Jim said. "We're all tired and hungry, so let's just calm down and try to figure out what to do. Heck, what Bob is saying is right. Legally we can't go into Mexico, especially to apprehend Mexican citizens. The other problem is that Juan Cortina has maybe fifty men riding for him, and I mean fifty killers. We're only three plus two kids. What kind of chance do you think we'd have?"

Heck backed away from Bob without taking his eyes off of him. He had no intention of stepping on his friend's authority, but he seemed to be the only one who clearly understood what had to be done. "I know what the dangers are, you don't have to tell me. I also know that none of us will feel good about letting them get away. We were able to beat the Comanche and we can beat these devils too, we just have to use our heads. Bob, I'm sorry. I didn't mean to question you, but I also know you, and we both know what has to be done. Juan Cortina and his gang come into our country to steal and murder, and then they slither back across the border like the snakes they are. They believe they can get away with it because of some darn line that we're not supposed to cross. They are cowards who make war on women and children, but hide from men. It just sticks in my craw that they use the law against us. Now they have murdered innocent townspeople and our own soldiers. They have also stolen the guns that we were assigned to recover, and they will use them to kill more of those we have sworn to protect. If we don't go after them now, then the blood of all those people will be on our hands, and I won't live with that on my conscience. Look Bob," Heck said in calmer tone, "I'll back your play, whatever you decide, just think about what I've said. This may be our last engagement as Texas Rangers, and if that's so, then I'd like to end it by doing our duty and locking them safely away in a Texas jail."

"Dang kid," Bob said with a smile, "with talk like that you should go into the legislature." Looking up at the sky, Bob thought about what to do. Turning back and going home was the logical choice, but was that really doing their duty? They all swore an oath to protect the citizens of Texas, and that would not be served by allowing Cortina and his bunch of killers to come back and kill more honest people whenever they had a mind to. "Jim, what are your thoughts?"

"I don't care to die in Mexico, or even to spend years locked away in one of their prisons. I don't think we can win this, we are five against Cortina's army. If his boys don't kill us, then we have the real army to worry about, and the Mexican government doesn't much care for Texians or the Rangers either. If they found us there they would lock us up and throw away the key." Jim looked at Heck, who looked back at him with an expression of disappointment, and Jim didn't like it. He appreciated the fact that the kid respected him and he didn't ever want that to change. Looking back at Bob, Jim finished by saying, "but I believe we have to go after them. The people they killed deserve justice, and besides, they've made me mad. They came into our camp and killed three young men under our protection, and that just don't sit right with me."

Bob nodded his head in agreement. "Well then, if we're going, we best get at it. Mathias, they were your pals that were killed. I suspect that you would want to go with us and help catch the men that done it."

Mathias knew he should want to go, as any one that considered himself a man would jump at the chance to get revenge on the ones that had killed their comrades. The truth was, he hadn't known those men that well, and they didn't really like him much anyway. The Rangers were all pretty much in agreement that they could not win a fight with this Cortina, and besides, there was one cannon left behind and it was his duty to get it back to General McCulloch. "I think I should get this cannon back to the army. General McCulloch will need all the artillery he can get. You don't really need me, so it would be better if I got back to the army and report what has happened here."

"I understand, son," Bob said.

168

Taking Tommy by the shoulder, he said, "Tommy, I want you to go back with Mathias and tell the Captain where we've gone."

Tommy pulled away from the older Ranger, "No sir. I'm going with ya'll. These are the ones that killed my family, and I intend to help bring 'em in."

He had never gone against anything that Bob Curtis had told him to do, and he didn't like having to do it now. Bob was the lead Ranger and that was a position that deserved respect, and Bob had certainly done enough to earn that respect, but this was something that Tommy felt he must do. He needed to settle this business, and one way or another, he wanted a showdown with Cortina. This was the reason that Tommy had stayed with the Rangers so long, to be there when Cortina was caught, and see him locked in a jail cell.

Bob shook his head. "Son, you need to do what I tell you," he said. "We don't stand much of a chance at this and I can't let them kill you too. That's not what your parents would want."

Tommy may have been young, but he was not stupid. He knew that four men against fifty would likely come out on the losing side, but he'd seen these Rangers come through tough scraps before, and figured they could make it through this as well. "Pardon me, but my parents are dead and it's up to me to get justice for 'em. I'd rather die trying to bring in their killers than to know I had the chance, but didn't do nothing."

Throwing his hands up in frustration, Bob gave up the argument. "Well dang, boys. I guess none of you are listening to me anymore. When we get back to San Antone we're gonna have a long talk about what it means to follow orders." Though Bob could hardly blame Tommy for seeking justice, he didn't like having his orders ignored. In the field, the men had to follow orders and Bob had no intention of letting this breach of authority stand, but that was a discussion that could wait for another time.

"Alright boy, you'll ride with us, but from here on out, you do exactly as you're told. If you get out of line once, you'd better learn to speak the language because I'll leave you in Mexico. You savvy what I'm saying?"

"Yes sir," Tommy said obediently. "I'll do whatever you say. You won't be sorry."

"Good enough," Bob said, although he figured they'd all be sorry before it was over. Speaking to everyone, he said, "I want y'all all to remember we're going there to apprehend them. We're about the law, not vengeance." Looking at each man in turn he assured himself that everyone heard what he said.

"Oliver," he said to the would-be lawman, "Is there someone in town who can help young Mathias get that cannon ready for transport?"

The man nodded his head. "We have a wheelwright. He's a drunk, but he should be able to get it fixed."

"Ok, good," Bob replied. "We'll also need some supplies. Do you think we could work out a line of credit with the general store? We don't have much hard cash, but the State of Texas will reimburse them for what we take."

A look of sadness came over the man's face as he said, "The Barton's owned the dry goods store, but they were two of the ones that Cortina's men killed. They shot them both to pieces for nothing." Considering the problem for a moment he said, "Under the circumstances, I don't reckon they'd mind extending a loan to you though."

With nothing left to be said, Bob climbed into the saddle. "Alright, let's go get our provisions and head out. I want us to make Matamoras before dark. With any luck, we'll find those skunks there and be back across the border by morning." Inside he felt it wouldn't be nearly that easy, but he didn't see the need in getting gloomy before they even started.

CHAPTER TWENTY-EIGHT

The summer had been dry in South Texas and the Rio Grande was only about fifty yards wide where the Rangers chose to make their crossing. The rocky bank sloped gently towards the water, giving way to soft earth near the bottom. All four men carefully coaxed their horses into the muddy water. River crossings were always dangerous, even shallow ones, like the Rio Grande.

Once in the water, the Rangers nudged the horses to a fast walk in order to avoid sinking into the muddy bottom. The currents were swift, and carried brush and other debris into the groups path. Even though the water was only a few feet deep, it was moving fast, and if anyone were to fall in, the current would carry them all the way into the Gulf of

Mexico. In just a few minutes they were on the Mexican side, and Bob lead the way up the trail towards Matamoras.

Matamoras was a haven for bandits and killers from both sides of the border, and the only law that applied was the one carried on the hip. The fastest and deadliest were in charge and everyone else either fell in line or were killed. The only rule that was enforced was that no one talked to the law under any circumstance, and the penalty for breaking this rule was a horrific death. Not only would their Ranger badges be useless here, it could very well get them killed. Even those who were not riding with Cortina would be a threat since he ran everything in this part of Mexico and would mete out rewards for those who helped him, as well as punishment for those that crossed him.

Riding into Matamoras, the four fanned out in different directions. The hope was to find Cortina and his men before they knew the Rangers were in town. Surprise would be the only advantage the four would have against the heavily armed and experienced militia.

The town was composed mainly of dilapidated adobe buildings, with a few wooden ones that appeared to be hastily constructed. There were two main streets that ran parallel to each other, and behind each was a narrow alley. Heck tied his horse in front of a water trough at the edge of town, where a few locals were milling about along the street. Most of the businesses were either boarded up or in such disrepair as to be considered unsafe by any civilized standards, so no one noticed as Heck made his way between two buildings to the alley in the rear.

Carefully peering around the corner, Heck looked down the alley in both directions, but saw nothing except trash and an old broken down wagon. Walking back to the street, he continued his search, trying to appear as if he were merely out for a stroll. He could hear the sounds of a large crowd coming from further down the street. The voices were coming from a cantina, in front of which were tied many horses, and Heck knew that if Cortina were still in town, that's where he would be found.

Smoke and the smell of sweat mixed with alcohol hung thick in the air as Heck approached the noisy cantina. He peered over the saloon doors, scanning the crowd for any sign that Cortina or his men were among the patrons. He had no idea what any of them looked like, but their kind would not be that hard to spot. Heck entered the cantina as if he belonged there, heading straight for the bar at the back of the room. Everyone was occupied with their own conversation, so no one gave him a second glance.

The burly bartender nodded his head in Heck's direction. "What you want, amigo?" He said. Heck propped his left foot on the rail, and used the mirror behind the bar to take another look around the room. Heck gave the bartender a hard look, judging him to be no better than those he served. Heck figured the man would cut his throat as quickly as anyone, if given half a chance. He decided he would keep one eye on him, no matter what.

"Amigo," the bartender repeated, "what do you want?"

"Tequila," Heck said. He watched as the man retrieved a bottle along with a glass and poured his drink, which he downed after slapping a coin onto the bar. Unless the bartender kept a poisoned bottle behind the bar for unwanted guests, Heck figured it was relatively safe to drink. Wiping his mouth on his sleeve, he asked for another, and while the bartender poured his shot, Heck decided it would be as good a time as any to ask about

Cortina. "Is Juan Cortina in town?" He said. "I'm looking for a job and thought he might be taking on hands."

"I pour drinks, not talk," he said. "You should go. You are not welcome here."

"Thank you for the information, amigo," Heck said, "and the drink."

Not wanting to get drunk, he slowly sipped his second drink, while carefully looking at everyone in the cantina. No one seemed to take any notice of him, which suited him just fine. He was at least fifty feet from the door, and didn't relish the thought of having to fight his way that far through a hostile crowd of armed bandits. He was planning all possible escape routes when out of the corner of his eye he saw a man approaching him from the far end of the bar. Without moving his head, Heck continued to follow the man's movement, sizing him up with every step. The would-be attacker was not a large man, but he walked with purpose and he was definitely concealing something in his right hand. He couldn't get a clear look at what he was holding, but felt safe in assuming it wasn't a bouquet of posies.

As carefully as he could, Heck released the rawhide thong that held his pistol in place, and placed his empty glass on the bar to be refilled. The man stopped a moment to see if Heck had noticed him, pretending to be looking for someone in the crowd. After assuring himself that he had not been noticed, he continued in Heck's direction.

The bartender finished pouring his drink and set the bottle down on the bar while he waited for payment. Heck turned around to face the bar, and saw that another few steps would put the man within his reach, unless of course, he chose to just shoot from where he stood.

The man took another step and brought up his concealed hand. Heck reached for his glass, but grabbed the half empty bottle of tequila instead, and as the attacker took one final step, Heck brought the bottle down on top of his head. The bottle shattered into pieces, covering both men with glass and the potent liquid.

Heck was now able to get his first clear look at the stranger, and was immediately glad he opted to use the bottle instead of trying to take him on with just his bare hands. While not tall, the man was barrel chested and had arms the size of tree trunks, and he most certainly had more experience at fisticuffs than Heck.

The blow from the bottle drove the man to his knees, causing the knife he carried in his right hand to fall to the floor. He quickly made it back to his feet and shook off the effects of the blow. Not wishing to see what his foe would do next, Heck drew his pistol and put the barrel to the man's head.

"Just hold it right there, friend," Heck said. "Who are you and why did you try to kill me?"

Wiping the blood from his head, the attacker replied, "My name's Humberto and I would kill you because you're the law, and because Cortina will pay very well for your head."

"Well Humberto, you and I are in a world of trouble," Heck said, looking around the cantina.

Everyone in the cantina were silently staring at the two men. Heck kept one eye on the crowd and the other on Humberto. He made up his mind that if they rushed him, he would shoot Humberto first and then take as many of the others as he could before they got him. He hoped it wouldn't come to that, but to make it out of the cantina alive would require some pretty quick talking on his part, or divine intervention. He hoped God was willing to do his part because he had never been much of a talker.

"Alright, let's not get excited," Heck said to the crowd, "I just want to talk to your friend here, and then I'll be on my way."

The crowd began to form a semi-circle around the two men, who were trapped between the bar and the angry mob. Heck kept his gun firmly pressed to Humberto's forehead, as he tried to think of a plan. "Okay, boys, I'm gonna walk out the door with this fella. I only want to talk to him, but if you try anything, he'll be the first to die, and a few of you will probably be joining him before you take me."

"We don't care nothing about him," someone yelled.

Another voice shouted, "Kill him then, but you'll never make it out of here alive."

A raucous chant of insults and threats then ensued from the crowd, which was so loud, that it was impossible to hear what was actually being said. Heck was beginning to get worried. The crowd was only a few feet away and could overpower him with very little effort, and they were either too mean, too drunk, or both, to care about the possibility of dying in the process. They wanted Heck dead and would not be satisfied with just talking about it for much longer. If Heck was going to make a move, it had to be now.

"I'm heading for the door," he said, "and if anybody tries to stop me, they'll die where they stand. There's no need for anyone to die today, so just step aside and let me and Humberto pass."

Slowly, he stepped forward and began making his way toward the door, and to his surprise the men standing in front of him moved out of the way. Walking past the sea of angry faces, Heck began to feel that he might actually make it out of the cantina with his skin. Only five feet from the door, he heard the unmistakable click of a hammer being pulled back, followed by a most unfriendly voice.

"I don't think so, senor. Go ahead and shoot Humberto if you want to. He'll probably be killed in the crossfire anyway. Now, I want you to turn around slowly so I can see your face as you die. I don't usually mind shooting a man in the back, but I think I'd like to watch a Texas Ranger suffer before he dies. Senor Cortina told us to kill you, but he didn't say we had to do it quick."

Heck stopped in his tracks, and let go of his prisoner. "Well Humberto, it looks like we both ran out of luck today." Heck took a deep breath and prepared to turn around. He wasn't sure where the man behind him was standing, so he figured he'd just have to turn around and start shooting, but before he could, he heard a familiar voice.

"Everybody hold it," Bob said, stepping into the room from the back door. In front of him stood the bartender, with Bob's shotgun pressed against his back.

"We've got all of you covered," Jim said, walking through the front door with Tommy, both with rifles in hand. "If anybody moves, we're all gonna start shooting and a whole lot of you will be leaving this saloon feet first."

"You okay, kid," Jim said, as he walked past his friend.

"I'm alright, Jim, but I'm sure glad to see you boys," Heck said, letting out a deep sigh. "I was afraid I was gonna have to shoot all of them myself, and you know how I hate a messy saloon."

Jim smiled, "I reckon we saved the lives of everyone of them."

"Whatcha doing with that fella, Heck?" Tommy said.

Heck smiled back at Tommy, "Well, it seems he was real anxious to meet me, and I figured we'd go outside to talk, where we could get a little peace and quiet."

"Amigos," Bob ordered, "I want everyone to drop their gun belts on the floor, and then we're all gonna head outside. Does everyone understand?"

No one said a word. They may have been out maneuvered, but they were still defiant.

"I asked if everyone understood," Bob said. "I want to see all heads nodding that you get what I'm saying." With these words, he raised his shotgun as if to fire.

While defiant, they were not about to challenge a shotgun. Obediently, they nodded their heads in unison, after which could be heard the sound of twenty guns hitting the ground.

With the barrel of his shotgun, Bob shoved the bartender forward. "Very good. Now that your teeth have been pulled, we'll step outside so that my friend and your friend can have a nice chat. The bartender will lead the way and everyone else will fall in line behind him, so let's get moving. I guess I don't need to say that if you try anything we'll start shooting."

With Bob, Jim, and Tommy following, the whole group walked out the door and into the street.

With the cantina to themselves, Heck set his prisoner into a chair and said, "I'm gonna ask nicely one time. Where can we find Juan Cortina?"

His head throbbing from being hit with a bottle, Humberto leaned back in his chair, and wiped the blood away from his wound. "I don't know where he is. I don't ride with him. Go back home gringo. You almost died here today and if you face Cortina you will not be so lucky."

Heck took a few breaths, trying to contain his temper. "Back home in Texas people usually respect law and order, and are happy to help us, but you and your friends don't respect laws or civilized behavior, so we have to be uncivilized. I asked one time nicely, just like I promised." Heck put his pistol to the man's head and pulled the hammer back. "This time I will not ask so nicely. You expected a reward for killing me, which means you knew where to go to collect. Where were you to go to collect your blood money? I want Cortina. I want him bad, and I will do whatever I have to in order to get him. You see, we don't have time to wait for him to come back to Texas, so I really need for you to help us find him." Tightening his fingers around the trigger he said, "I will not ask again."

Humberto knew as well as anyone that talking to the law was an automatic death sentence in Matamoras, but at the moment, not talking would mean an even quicker death. He had assumed that Heck's threat was a bluff, just so much hot wind, but one look into the Ranger's eyes told a different story. "Hidalgo. He's in Hidalgo. It's a two days' ride south of here."

"Thank you," Heck replied, putting his pistol back in its holster. "Now, if I were you, I'd high tail it outta here and not come back. It won't take your friends long to figure out you talked to me."

A few miles outside of town, the Rangers let the bandits' horses loose. "Those outlaws will spend the next two days looking for their horses," Bob said. "By then, we'll be in Hidalgo, and up to our neck in fresh problems."

"You don't think we can win, do you Bob?" Heck said.

"I don't know, kid. We really have no idea how many men Cortina has riding with him. It could be ten, it could be fifty, but we do know that they are all experienced killers and they enjoy it. To win, we will have to be as brutal as they are if we even make it to Hidalgo."

It had never occurred to Heck that they would not reach Hidalgo. "What do you mean if we make Hidalgo?"

"There could be Federales on the road, and if there are, they would probably be on Cortina's payroll. The good news is, they would just turn us over to Cortina to be killed, instead of taking us to prison." Bob paused a moment to survey the trail with his spyglass. "I'll ride ahead a few miles and scout the road. If I see anyone, I'll try to make it back to warn you. Jim, you make sure the group stays behind me a few miles. I'll see y'all when we make camp."

The sun was just beginning to rise when the Rangers stopped to get a few hours sleep. It was only through shear grit that they had made it this far, but that had carried them as far as it was going to, and now they had to rest, or risk dropping from total exhaustion.

They chose a small stand of trees just off the trail to make their camp, and Bob rode back to join them. All were asleep a few moments after closing their eyes.

CHAPTER TWENTY-NINE

"Wake up kid, it's almost noon and Jim has breakfast going," Bob said, nudging Heck with his boot. "We gotta get moving."

The morning was already hot, and promised to get much hotter. A steaming cup of coffee helped to bring the men back to life, and that, along with a few strips of fat back and a hoe cake, was the first civilized meal the men had eaten in days. Bob wolfed his food down while standing, and quickly worked to saddle his horse.

"Just like yesterday, I'll ride a few miles ahead and y'all will keep pace behind me. With a little luck, we will reach the town by daybreak," Bob said, swinging into the saddle.

In a few minutes, they were back on the trail. Jim turned around in his saddle and said, "Remember boys, if anybody asks, we're ranchers who crossed the border to buy some cheap cattle, so try to look like ranchers."

"What do ranchers look like?" Tommy asked, shoving the last piece of bacon into his mouth. Jim said nothing, but shot him a look that conveyed his annoyance.

Continuing, Jim said, "From here on we must be careful. If Cortina really is in Hidalgo, the chances are pretty high that he will have lookouts on the road into town. Once there, we must all stay alert. If our rouse doesn't work, we may have to fight our way out. If that happens, we will rendezvous back at this campsite and cross the border together. Does everyone understand?"

His question went unanswered but all were aware of the plan, as well as the dangers looming on the horizon.

"Okay then, from here on out, we are just Texas ranchers," Jim said.

For the better part of a day, the Rangers rode with hardly a word spoken between them. Each man was too busy with their own thoughts, which they did not want to give voice to.

Upon arriving in Hidalgo, the Rangers were surprised by how quiet it was. Other than a few elderly men sitting in rocking chairs, the town seemed completely deserted. The silence was broken only occasionally by the sound of roosters crowing in the distance.

There was only one street in town, which was bounded by a mission on one end and an old hotel at the other. The sun reflected off the broken windows of the dilapidated structures in multi-colored prisms, which made it hard to see what was in front of them as they ambled along the street.

The men reined in their horses outside of what appeared to serve as both café and cantina. As they dropped off their mounts, each man scoured the street, but seeing nothing they continued walking to the door.

Bob turned to Heck and said, "Heck, I want you and Tommy to wait out here while we talk to the proprietor of this fine establishment. Be sure and keep your eyes open. If anything is going to happen, I would rather it be out in the open where we can reach the horses."

Sitting down in a couple of wooden chairs, Heck and Tommy waited on the others to get the information they needed.

"It doesn't look like Cortina is here. There's no horses tied up on the street and they would have to be traveling with several wagons to haul the guns and cannon. Right?" Tommy said.

"What did you say, Tommy?" Heck asked, glancing down the street in both directions.

"I said, it doesn't seem like Cortina and his men are here."

"Don't be fooled by the quiet, kid. A wise man once told me to always pay attention to that which seems out of place, and it's not normal for a town to be this quiet."

In a few minutes, Bob and Jim walked out, and both had a look of uncertainty. Bob shielded his eyes from the sun as he looked around the desolate town. "The owner says he hasn't seen Cortina for a long time, and assumed he was still across the border. The deep ruts I saw back on the trail tells me something different. Someone came through here in the last couple of days with several wagons, and judging by the depth of those ruts, the wagons were loaded with something very heavy. He did tell us that a man that works for Cortina comes in every morning for breakfast, and he suggests that we wait and talk to him."

"Do you trust him?" Heck asked.

"Hell no, I don't trust him. But the way I see it, we have to wait and see how this thing plays out. Just be ready for anything," Bob said.

Jim paced the wooden sidewalk, which creaked loudly with every step. "Heck," he said, "Why don't you and Tommy take a little walk around town and see what you can find?"

"Will do. Keep a sharp eye while we're gone," Heck said.

Heck and Tommy walked down the middle of the deserted street. The windblown sand stung their faces, and it was all but impossible to concentrate on the surroundings.

Thinking it would be quicker to split up Heck said, "Tommy, you walk along and look inside some of these buildings while I keep heading up to the mission. If they're here, they would have to be hiding inside somewhere."

The church was by far the newest and nicest structure in town, and its red adobe façade stood in stark contrast to the ramshackle condition of every other building. The sun reflected off the brass bell that hung in the bell tower some thirty feet above the street.

Heck squinted against the brightness to get a look inside the tower, but the reflection was too blinding for him to make out anything other than an orange blur. Remembering once again the advice of Old Tom, Heck did not like the fact that he hadn't seen one horse since they rode into town. There was not one in the corral or tied to any of the hitching posts, and he found this very much out of the ordinary. Tom's advice had saved him more times than the Colt he wore on his hip and he wasn't about to ignore it now.

Heck walked to the back of the church and peered inside the door, which led to a courtyard. In the middle of the courtyard stood a fountain with a statue of the Virgin Mary in the center. He paused just inside the door and listened, but heard nothing.

He searched from one end of the courtyard to the other, but it appeared the church was as deserted as the rest of the town. Removing his bandana, he dipped it into the fountain and wiped the dirt and grime of the trail from his face and neck, and the cool water felt good against the already sweltering morning heat. The respite put his mind at ease, but as he raised his head to let the water run down his neck, he was able to see into the back of the belfry. With the back of the tower in shadows, he caught the form of someone moving under the bell. It was probably the parish priest, but Heck couldn't help thinking that it would be the perfect place for a rifleman to wait in ambush for four unsuspecting Texas Rangers.

Heck found the wooden steps leading up the belfry, and after removing his boots, he made his way up to the top of the tower. There was no air movement in the tower and halfway up he felt as though he might pass out from exhaustion. Sweat poured down his face and stung his eyes, causing him to pause so he could wipe his face and catch his breath.

After resting a moment, he sprinted the rest of the way up. A trap door led into the bell tower and Heck carefully opened it and looked inside. He saw a young Mexican man with a rifle keeping a careful eye on the street below.

Heck did not want to give away his presence, so he decided to use his knife rather than his pistol. The man was about ten feet away and it would be difficult to reach him before he could bring the Sharps rifle to bare. There was also a very good possibility the man was carrying a pistol, but as Heck did not have any other options, he eased his way through the narrow trap door. Standing up in the belfry, he tightened his grip around the handle of the bowie knife and leapt at the rifleman. The man wheeled around with his rifle as Heck landed on his back, but it was a fruitless gesture. There was a look of pained surprise on the man's face as Heck covered his mouth and pulled him to the floor. Heck plunged his knife into the man's chest several times, as he kept his hand over the man's mouth. After several seconds his muffled cries were silent.

"We've got problems, boys," Heck said, upon entering the café.

Bill drew his pistol and went to the window to survey the street. "What's going on, kid?"

"We're being setup for an ambush. I just took out a rifleman up in the church steeple, but I'd bet a week's wages that he's not alone. A sharp shooter at one end of the street might get a couple of us, but to be assured of killing us all, they would need one at the other end of the street as well.

"I looked in all the buildings and I didn't see anyone," Tommy said.

Jim sat at a table by the window, with his rifle laid across his lap. "There's no one moving out there at all. If they're waiting to gun us, they're keeping themselves hidden."

"Doesn't that strike anybody else as strange. A whole town and nobody on the streets or in the stores," Heck said, as he secured the café's back door.

Jim walked over to the café owner, and grabbed him by the shirt. "I guarantee he knows where they're hiding. Don't you, amigo. You'd better go ahead and tell us where. You don't seem like the sort who holds with Cortina's methods. Why are you helping them?"

The café owner looked at the floor for a moment before answering, "Cortina and his men run this town, and many more just like it. He is very powerful and has friends in the government and the army. There are many honest people in Hidalgo, but we are not fighters and we are scared for our families."

Jim nodded his understanding. He had seen this kind of thing many times, and knew that all the honest people needed was a reason to stand up for themselves. "We intend to arrest Cortina and his men and take them back to Texas. If you help us, you will be rid of them and have your town back, but if you don't, if they are successful in killing us, you will be under their boot forever and so will your children."

"There is no way you will be able to defeat Cortina," the owner said. "He has too many men and they are all muy malo. Very bad. I wish you would go back where you came from. You all seem like good men and I would not wish to see you killed in such a foolish attempt, but if you will not listen to wisdom, I can at least help you in this small way. Besides the one your friend killed, there is one on the fourth floor of the hotel at the other end of the street, and there are four more in the livery stable across the street. They are waiting for all of you to walk out into the street together, and then they plan on killing you all at once."

"Well gentlemen," Bob said. "What do you want to do? If we go out into the street, we will be cut down for sure, but if we stay here, they will grow tired of waiting on us and will simply lay siege and starve us out."

"As I see it," Heck said, "we only have one option and that is to turn the tables and kill them before they can kill us. I've been thinking on a plan and if it works I will be able to drive them into the street and all you'll have to do is take care of them once they show themselves." Heck reached into a small wooden box on the bar and pulled out a handful of matches, and then retrieved two bottles of tequila from behind the bar.

"What's your plan, Heck?" Jim said.

"I don't have it all figured out yet, but I will shortly. Just stay by the window and all three of you be ready to start shooting."

Jim reached out and grabbed Heck's arms as he walked to the back door. "You don't have to do this on your own."

"Yes I do, Jim. For this to work, I am counting on y'all to handle things here on the street. Don't worry, I have no intention of letting this band of killers take me. I'll be darned if I'll give 'em that satisfaction." Giving his friends a wave and smile, he left the café through the back door.

Once at the back of the livery, Heck was glad to see there was no guard posted. There was, however, an old cart containing several bales of hay, which he pushed in front of the rear door and then doused with half a bottle of tequila. He then doused the door and back wall with the remaining bottle and a half and lit a match. The liquor quickly ignited, and as the orange flames licked the air, Heck ran off toward the hotel.

There was a narrow alley that ran between the hotel and the abandoned building next door, and Heck carefully maneuvered around the old crates and other assorted trash to reach the back of the hotel. He entered through the back door and made his way to the empty lobby, which was even more eerily quiet than the street outside. Looking out the front door, he could see that the smoke from the livery was rising at least fifty feet into the air. The street was still deserted, so Heck assumed that the fire had not yet spread through the building. "Good," Heck thought. "Hopefully I can make it to the fourth floor before the mayhem starts."

Halfway up the third flight of stairs, Heck was wishing someone else had volunteered for this mission. He was the one having to climb all the stairs, while the rest of them were sitting in a nice cool saloon.

Making his way to the fourth floor, he slowly peeked his head around the corner and looked down the hallway in both directions. The stairs were covered in an ornate red carpet, which he hoped had muffled the sound of his footsteps. The café owner didn't know which room the gunman was in, only that it was in a room on the top floor. Heck knew he had to be in a room on the right side of the hall, as these were the only ones with a view of the street. Stopping at the first door, Heck listened, but could hear no sound coming from within, so he tiptoed towards the next door. He had only taken a few steps when gunshots broke the silence on the street below.

Heck rushed to the next door and turned the doorknob, but it was locked. Backing up a few feet, he threw himself at the door, hitting it with his shoulder. The door jamb broke easily, allowing the door to swing open, and Heck landed on the floor inside the room. Victor stood at the window with a Henry rifle, and he quickly turned around and leveled the rifle at Heck, but he wasn't quick enough. Victor saw a muzzle flash as Heck fired at him three times, but the outlaw was dead before the second shot hit his body.

"Here they come," Bill shouted.

Four men ran out into the street, each covering their mouth with one hand, and shooting wildly with the other. A short, stocky Mexican was the first to fall, felled by a lead ball right between the eyes.

The other three jumped behind a trough, taking cover from the torrent of shot unleashed by the three men.

"They think that trough will protect them," Tommy laughed. "We'll shoot it to pieces, and them with it."

Bob knelt down to reload his pistol. "I'd rather not use up what little ammunition we have on some dang horse trough. Cortina has a small army riding with him, so I doubt this will be our last gun battle. We'd do better waiting them out. They can't stay there forever, and I promise you we're a lot more comfortable than they are right now."

A shot rang out, striking one of the men crouched behind the trough. He made it to his feet and tried running for better cover, but only made it a couple of feet before a second shot knocked him to the ground.

Jim smiled. "Looks like Heck was able to get rid of the other rifleman. Those shots came from down the street, and from a rifle."

The other two gunmen came out from their hiding place, firing at both the hotel and the café. It was a futile move made by desperate men, one the Rangers might have chosen if their roles had been reversed.

"Keep firing, boys. We got 'em caught in a crossfire," Jim said.

Both men were cut down where they stood, their bodies riddled with holes.

191

With the end of the gunfire, people started appearing out nowhere, buckets in hand, to put out the flames before they spread to the whole town. The Rangers felt obliged to pitch in and help put out the fire, and were amazed at how fast the townspeople worked, and how quickly the flames were extinguished.

With the danger over, the café owner told them where to find Cortina's ranch, and even drew them a map of the best route to take. There were two routes into the ranch, but he advised them to take the mountain pass. It would take longer than the other route because it required them to cross through the Sierra de Tamaulipas Mountains, but it would allow them to reach the ranch unseen. He told them that there was a narrow, but passable trail that led over the mountain and onto the ranch, and it was unlikely that any sentries would be posted along this route. With map in hand, but with no clear idea of what to do once they arrived, the four set out for the reckoning that all saw looming on the horizon.

Tommy felt a great deal of satisfaction seeing those gunmen die in Hidalgo. He couldn't be sure that any of them had been present when his family was killed, as he only remembered one of the killers, but they were certainly responsible for similar atrocities against other families. It made little difference to him. The men they had killed in Hidalgo were the same as the butchers who had killed his family and it felt good to see them get their comeuppance. He knew the Captain and Old Tom would not approve of these feelings, and they would point out how the Bible teaches forgiveness and love for one's enemies. They would undoubtedly remind him that as Texas Rangers, they were expected to uphold the law and to never let their personal feelings interfere with the job. Tommy believed in what the Bible taught and he tried very hard to follow God's Commandments, but he couldn't help how he felt inside. He would never pray for anyone's death, but if Cortina and his men were to die horribly, Tommy would not pretend to feel bad about it.

CHAPTER THIRTY

Cortina's ranch was about a day's ride to the southwest by the mountain route. As had been the norm on this mission, the four men said little as they rode through the night. The sparsely forested grasslands gave way to rocky terrain as they made their accent up the mountain.

"Cortina may be a thieving butcher," Jim said, "but he certainly knows how to pick the right place for a ranch. This mountain would make a formidable obstacle in the event of attack."

Bob laughed. "That doesn't bode very well for us then, does it?"

"I was talking about ordinary men, not four rough cobs like us."

Heck turned up the collar of his shirt for protection from the cold as they climbed to higher altitude. He thought about the events of the last several weeks, and the final battle that was yet to come. So far they had been extremely lucky. The mob in Matamoras and the ambush in Hidalgo could have ended very differently, had providence not stepped in to save them. Even though they had some extremely close calls, those they had defeated so far were gunmen that Cortina was willing to sacrifice and felt were easily replaced. When they reached the ranch, they would be facing the best of Cortina's killers, men who enjoyed killing and were very experienced in battle. The Rangers were only three in number, with an inexperienced sixteen-year-old boy thrown in for good measure. Heck, Jim, and Bob had fought in numerous engagements against brutal killers. They had faced Comanche, Mexican bandits, cattle thieves, and slavers, all of whom were desperate killers and never went down without a fight. Cortina and his men were different. They were large in number, smart, and the Rangers would be fighting them on their own terrain. Cortina also had the backing of the local Mexican militia, who were no friends of the Texas Rangers. Taken as a whole, Heck didn't give them a snowball's chance in hell of making it back alive.

The outlaw's ranch was set in a deep valley between two rocky outcroppings. The green pastures were periodically interrupted by small stands of Mexican Buckeye and even at two-thousand feet, their vivid purple flowers were magnificent. The Rangers looked down from a plateau suspended above the lush green earth below. The red rocky cliffs formed shear walls that ran all the way to the base of the small canyon. Only one trail could be seen, a narrow path between the red wall and the open air to nowhere.

Jim had hoped to see more than one path to the bottom. One trail meant that it would be guarded by at least one sentry.

"I don't like this at all," Jim said. "They're sure to have a lookout posted."

Bob scanned the vista with his spyglass, careful to keep a sharp eye out for any movement or anything out of place. "I don't feel good about it either, Jim," Bob said, "but there's no other trail within a day's ride. I guess this is why Cortina feels so secure here." Taking another look through his spyglass, he hoped to see something, anything. "I don't see anybody, which means they're very well hidden. That trail has so many twists and turns, a whole army could be hiding down there and we'd never spot 'em til it was too late."

The four stood, staring down the trail, looking for nothing in particular, but none of them was eager to proceed. They all knew there was no turning back, but once they started down the mountain trail they would have to admit that to themselves.

Heck eased his appaloosa forward until he was parallel with Tommy's horse. Heck reached out and put his hand on the young man's shoulder. "I want you to stay in the rear on the way down. If anything goes wrong, you need to get out of there quick. We'll do our best to fight them off and give you time to get away. You ride hard and fast, and try to find a good place to hold up. Travel at night and stay outta sight during the day. If you keep heading north, you'll eventually make your way back across the border. You get what I'm saying? Look at me. You hear me?"

Tommy nodded his head. "Yeah Heck. I hear ya."

"Good. See that you do it," Heck said.

Walking his horse to the trail head, Heck turned to the others and said, "Well boy's, we'd better get moving. Cortina's not going to arrest himself." Jim took the lead, followed by Bob, then Heck, and as instructed Tommy brought up the rear.

A few hundred yards down the trail the slope increased, causing the horses to slip occasionally on the slick surface. With no experience in mountainous terrain, Tommy's first instinct was to tighten up on the reins, in an effort to slow his horse down.

"Give him his head," Heck said, without looking back, "Your horse will find his footing on his own."

The trail was just wide enough for one horse, leaving a little room for the horses to navigate around the fallen rock that littered their path. Bob, who hated heights, did everything he could to avoid looking to his right, and the immediate drop into the abyss.

After a few hours, the group was close to reaching the bottom. The red rock was being replaced by a reddish-brown dirt, and sweet acacia could be seen popping up between the cracks in the rocky face of the mountain. Closing in on their objective had not lightened Jim's mood. He pulled his Sharps from its boot and laid it across his saddle's pommel, resting the barrel in the crook of his free arm. "Look sharp, boys," he said. "We're almost back on solid ground and Cortina's boys could show up anywhere."

In front of them, the trail turned left into one of the many switchbacks, and Jim and Bob disappeared around the bend. Almost immediately after losing sight of his comrades, Heck was deafened by the sound of several gunshots reverberating off the rocky walls of the mountain. Shaking off the ringing in his ears, Heck pulled his colt and spurred his horse to a trot. Rounding the bend, Heck was prepared for anything, anything that is, except for what he found.

The bodies of two men lay on the ground, and Heck froze for a moment, trying to make up his mind whether to go after the one's responsible, or to stay and offer aid to his fellow Rangers.

Climbing off his horse, Heck knelt down next to Bob. His shirt was red with blood, and Heck recognized instantly it was too late. Ranger Captain Bob Curtis was gone. He then walked over to the body of Jim, and judging from the pool of blood collecting around his head, there would be no saving his other friend either. Heck gently rolled the man's body over, just to be sure, and was shocked beyond words to see it was not Jim's body after all. Whoever the dead man was, he must have been killed by Jim, because Bob's gun was still in his holster. He figured there must have been two sentries posted, and Jim had ridden after the other man.

Turning back to the body of Ranger Curtis, all his feelings were washed away in a flood of overwhelming loss, and if there was one thing he had learned in all his years as a Ranger, it was loss.

Old Tom had always told him that Rangering was a dangerous life, and if you survived doing it for more than five years, you were beating the odds. Heck had been with Company C a few months shy of nine years, and in that time the company had lost five good men. Heck knew that Old Tom was right; this life was all about loss.

Tommy had followed Heck's instructions, and lit out when the gunfire started. Spurring his horse on as fast as he dared, he ascended back up the mountain and then took the first trail he found that headed north. He felt guilty about leaving his friends to their inevitable death, but he felt worse about letting his family down. He had stood over their graves and sworn he would avenge them no matter the cost, and now he had run away when he was close to actually seeing justice done for them.

Reining his horse to a stop, he tried to catch his breath and gave careful thought to what he would do next. Heck had ordered him to head back to Texas, and the order made sense. After all, he was just a boy and what help could he possibly be to the Rangers. He would just be in their way. Yes, he decided, he would get back across the border and wait. If the Rangers failed, Cortina and his men would come back there sometime soon and he and his family would have their justice then. Tommy would use the time to practice with his gun. He would become fast and accurate. He would become faster than Jim or Heck, and he would be ready when the killers made their return to Texas.

Heck heaved Bob's body onto the back of his horse and hurried down the trail in search of Jim. If the man Jim was pursuing made it back to the rest of the gang, all would be lost. The only chance the Rangers had was to somehow take Cortina by surprise, which would be a challenge under the best of circumstances. Heck did not want Bob's sacrifice to have been in vain, but neither did he come all this way to have himself and Jim die in a suicide attack on Cortina.

Checking both sides of the trail for any sign of Jim, Heck resigned himself to the fact that survival might mean having to leave Cortina and his bunch for another day. Heck hated to lose, and the idea of giving up infuriated him, but his quest had already cost one Ranger his life, and he had no intention of sacrificing another.

Heck caught site of a rider approaching him from the opposite direction. Pulling his rifle out, he positioned his sites on the man's midsection and waited for the unknown rider to come into full view. If he was anyone other than Jim, Heck would drop him in hurry.

It was Jim, and Heck greeted his friend with a warm smile. "I'm glad to see you, Jim. I wasn't sure if you had made it." Jim had a look of sadness such as Heck had seldom seen on any man, let alone Jim King. He looked right past Heck to the body of their fallen comrade.

"I wasn't fast enough, Heck. We went around that bend and rode right up on them bushwhackers. I fired quick and got one of 'em, but I couldn't kill the other one before he got off a shot. I could tell it was bad for Bob, but I knew I had to get the other man before he made it back to Cortina. After he shot Bob, I fired and got him in the side, I think. I lit out down the trail, and made it just beyond that stand of trees over there," he said, pointing over his shoulder. "He fell off his horse and I finished him off with my knife. I wanted to see him die slow for what he done, but I knew there might be more of them about. I wanted to kill him bad, Heck. That's a feeling I thought I had seen the last of, but after Bob, it came right back."

Heck looked at Bob's body and said, "I'm sorry about Bob, Jim. You've known him longer than me, but he was my friend too. It looks like the shot caught him in the heart, so I don't suspect he suffered any."

"Where's Tommy?" Jim said.

"I told him if anything happened, he should get out as fast as he could and make for the border."

Jim nodded his head, but seemed lost in thought. "That's probably what we should do as well. It's just the two of us now, and we don't stand a chance against Cortina's boys. We've killed some of his men, but you can bet he's kept his best fighters back, waiting for us to get close to him. He may have ten or more men left, and while you and I are fierce, we're not that good. We should find a nice spot to bury Bob, lay low until dark, and then head for home."

Digging Bob's grave took the better part of two hours and the sun had almost disappeared behind the mountains when they carefully lowered the body and began to cover it up with the soft earth.

Removing his hat, Heck wiped the sweat from his forehead. Taking a deep breath, he asked, "Do you want to say a few words, Jim?"

"No, kid. You've got a better handle on words than I do. You say something."

Heck bowed his head and tried to remember some of the words he had heard preachers say at times like these. "Lord we offer prayer that you will bless this man and forgive him anything he may have done against—" Choking up a bit, Heck paused for a moment, thinking about what to say. "Lord we give you the body of our friend and comrade in arms. He was a man, no better or worse than any other, but he was a brave and true Ranger. He will be missed."

Both men put their hats back on and silently walked back to their horses.

Climbing into the saddle, Heck said, "I don't feel right about riding out without finishing what we came here for. I want to go get Cortina or die trying."

A huge grin grew from the sides of Jim's mouth and he said, "I'm glad to hear you say that, kid. I was fixin' to suggest the same thing."

CHAPTER THIRTY-ONE

Jim and Heck checked their armaments before heading down the trail to Cortina's ranch house. Both men had two pistols with twelve rounds of shot and powder each, plus they each had their Sharps rifles. They would assuredly be outmanned and outgunned, but Jim hoped that the element of surprise and a good battle plan would even the odds a bit.

"Let's move out, kid," Jim said. "It could still be quite a fair peace to their ranch house. If they don't already know we're here, they should be indoors by the time we arrive. If we're real lucky, they might be asleep, or even drunk."

Heck gave him a wave and swung into the saddle. "Yeah, if we sit around too long thinking about it, we're liable to talk ourselves out of it."

"We wouldn't want good sense to cloud our judgment," Jim said with a chuckle.

It took Heck and Jim more than two hours to reach Cortina's house, which actually consisted of several structures. There was a low stone building with a large chimney rising up through the center of the roof, which was undoubtedly the kitchen and mess. To the left was a larger structure made of wood planks, with heavy wooden shutters covering the windows, and a porch ran all the way across the front and half way down both sides. The porch was covered with a shingled roof, which was supported with hewn logs. From the size of it, the Rangers assumed this was probably the bunk house. Fifty yards to the right of the kitchen was a large two-story stone house, made of limestone and granite. Like the bunk house, the windows of the main house were covered with shutters. It was very well fortified, with a heavy wooden front door, which was supported with thick, wrought iron hinges. This was by far the nicest of the three structures, and there no doubt that Juan Cortina would be found behind its solid, wood door.

Crouched down under a large pecan tree, and looking at their target, the two Rangers discussed what needed to be done. It was a cloudless night, with a three-quarter moon, so the grounds surrounding the houses were well lit.

Jim stared at the main house for some time before speaking. "That's a big heavy door. I won't be able to break it down by myself. Even if we both put our weight into it, I don't think we could get through it."

"What do you suggest we do?" Heck asked.

"Well, if we can't get through the door, we'll have to get Cortina to open it and let us in."

Heck thought a moment, and then an idea came to him. "In Hidalgo, I got those gunmen to come out to us. There's no reason that the same thing wouldn't work here."

"You're talking about lighting the house?" Jim asked.

"Don't tell me you're squeamish about burning out a bunch of rats," Heck said.

Jim shook his head. "No. We're the law and that has to mean something. There's got to be a line that we won't cross. You did what had to be done in Hidalgo because they were trying to bushwhack us, but this time we're in control. I intend to give them the chance to surrender, and if they refuse, then so be it."

"I understand what you're saying," Heck said, "but these are bad men and you know as well as I do that we're gonna get bloody."

Jim knew his friend was right. He might have been Heck's mentor, but there was nothing left that he could teach him. Heck was a natural at Rangering, and had an instinct for how to play any given situation, but Jim could still try to impart some wisdom to his younger friend. Heck had more courage and fight than any five men that Jim had ever known, but he also had a single mindedness when it came to his sense of right and wrong. Jim wouldn't say that Heck was careless, but he lived for the fight, and fought with a blind rage when he knew he was in the right.

Jim pointed toward their objective, and said, "You take the bunk house and I'll take Cortina in the main house. I'll try to make some noise and get him to open the door, and then I'll take him."

Slapping Jim on the back, Heck said, "Sounds easy. We'll be enjoying biscuits and coffee around the campfire before we know it." Heck grabbed Jim by the shirt and pulled him to the other side of the tree. He squinted against the brightness of the moon, trying to focus on an object in the distance. Through the blackness, Heck made out the form of an approaching rider. "Jim," Heck said, "there's a rider coming this way."

The Rangers laid flat on the ground as Jim lined up the stranger in his rifle sites. They were on a slight incline and hidden behind the large tree. From this position, Jim knew he would easily be able to dispatch the rider, even as poor as he was with a rifle.

Watching the figure approach, Heck thought there was something familiar in the horse's gait, as it trotted with a bit of a stutter step. Coming out of the shadows, the rider was now fully engulfed in moonlight, and both Rangers let out a sigh of relief. Jim stood up and motioned for Tommy to dismount and join them.

"Ya darn fool," Heck said, "I thought I told you to ride for home."

"I did what you said. I was halfway to back to Brownsville, but I decided to come back and lend you fellas a hand," Tommy said. "I got to thinkin' how this is more my fight than yours, and it weren't right for me to just run away. So here I am."

"I don't mean to interrupt your little confab, but if we're gonna do this, we'd better get on with it," Jim said.

Heck looked at Tommy, trying to decide how to proceed. "Okay, Jim. How do you want to play this?"

"I'll take Tommy with me. I bet he'll make a good diversion, if I'm in need of one."

Heck watched the bunk house for twenty minutes before he saw the opportunity he had been waiting for. The door to the house opened and a short, squatty man stepped out onto the porch. He paused a moment, scanning the perimeter, before continuing to the outhouse, which was only about twenty feet behind the bunkhouse.

When Heck saw the privy door close, he made a beeline for the rear of the bunkhouse. He crouched down and listened for anyone else who might be answering the call of nature, but hearing nothing he stood up and moved along the shadows.

He crept to the side of the outhouse, so that when the door opened he would be concealed until the last possible moment.

A velvet blanket of clouds rolled in from the west and completely obscured the moon. It would make the task at hand easier, but would also make it harder to detect anyone who might be hiding in the shadows. The stiff breeze that brought the clouds had turned the night air cool, but with his adrenaline pumping, Heck hardly noticed.

Drawing his knife, Heck knelt in the dirt as the privy door swung open. He griped the stag handle of his bowie tighter, trying to focus the abundance of energy coursing through his body. Heck knew that the worst thing to do in these situations was to move too fast, so he resisted the urge to attack. He had to take this man quickly and quietly, so the others would not be alerted to the impending attack.

As the man closed the privy door, Heck grabbed him around the neck and forced him to the ground. He was much stronger than he looked and fought with everything he had to reach the gun on his hip. Heck had to drop his knife in order to grab the man's arm with his free hand, while keeping his other arm around the man's throat. His grip was not enough, and the outlaw's fingers wrapped around the handle of his pistol. The man lurched forward and then fell onto his back, pinning Heck underneath him. Heck loosened his grip on the outlaw's throat, who quickly rolled off him with his gun in hand, but Heck had already retrieved his knife, and reaching behind the man's head, he drove it into the base of his skull. His body stiffened for just a second before going limp.

Heck drew his pistols and crept along the side of the house, stopping to assure himself that no one had heard the scuffle. Hearing nothing, he stepped around the corner, and right into the path of a very large gentleman hurrying to the outhouse. It would be difficult to say who was more surprised, as they both took a step back and froze in place.

The man was huge, but what struck Heck the most about his appearance, was the enormous scar that ran across the man's face. Drunk and barely able to stand, the man had to catch his balance on the porch railing, giving Heck the chance he needed. Leaping forward, Heck raised his pistol and brought it down on top of the big man's head, but unfortunately his head was covered with an even bigger hat, which absorbed the blow. Heck was about to hit him again, when the door to the bunk house opened and a booming voice from inside called out, "Hey Guillermo, before you drain it, how about loaning me some dinero so I can sta—" The sight of Guillermo getting buffaloed stopped the man in midsentence.

There was no decision to make this time. Without hesitation, Heck pulled the hammer back on both pistols and fired. The man would no longer have need for that dollar.

The blow to the head sobered Guillermo up, but as he started to rise, Heck hit him twice more. The big man sunk to the ground without a sound.

Heck gave no thought to what would happen next, as he coolly walked through the door of the bunkhouse firing both guns. Three men were sitting at a small table in the middle of the room, and were the next to fall.

The bunk house consisted of one room lined with cots and a smaller room to the right of the door. The stale smell of cheap whiskey and tobacco permeated the cramped living quarters.

An old, dirty man with a limp tried to make for the small room, and if not for the limp, he might have made it. As it turned out, the Comanche brave who gave him the limp ended up killing him after all, even if he hadn't lived to see it.

Multiple shots shattered the door behind Heck. A couple of brave men made a valiant effort to save their own lives, but courage alone never won the day. Heck possessed the necessary quality which they lacked; a cool head under fire. It was something that couldn't be taught or learned, you were either born with it or you weren't. The two continued firing wildly as Heck walked towards them, as though he was enjoying a Sunday stroll. When he was within five feet of his targets, he fired one shot from each Colt.

Jim peered through the window of the kitchen, and saw an old Mexican man and a boy of about twelve washing dishes. The Ranger slipped through the door and put his gun to the old cook's head. "Don't make a sound, amigo. Do you speak English?"

The old man nodded his understanding.

"Good," Jim said, "That will make this much easier. I'm a Texas Ranger and my companions and I are here for Juan Cortina and his militia. We're not after you or the boy, but we could use your help. If you help us, we'll finish our business and be on our way, but if you want to take Cortina's part, I'll end you right now."

208

"Si, I will help you," he said.

"Okay. What I want you to do will only take a moment and will be very easy."

"Si, what can I do?"

"How many men does Cortina have in the main house with him?" Jim asked.

"There is only one man with Senor Cortina. His name is Zapata, and he's muy malo, just like Cortina," He said.

"Good. You and the boy will help me get inside the house and then you're done. We'll take Cortina and then go." Jim said. "What's your name?"

"My name is Cerra," he said.

"Well Cerra," he said, "Let's get this done."

From the side of the house, Jim watched Cerra and the boy approach the front door. The plan was simple, Cerra and the boy would get Cortina to open the door, and then Jim would rush inside and capture him. It was simple, but by no means assured of succeeding. If things went wrong, Cerra and the boy would be caught in the cross-fire, but it was the best plan they could come up with on short notice.

Hearing the knock at the door, Zapata rose from the chair where he was cleaning his shotgun. It was not unusual for one of the men to come by the house at a late hour, but Cortina had given strict orders not to be bothered this evening. Zapata was a man totally without fear, and this was mainly due to the fact that he was always prepared for anything.

With pistol in hand, Zapata walked to the door, and opened the small gun slit and looked out to see who had stupidly disobeyed Cortina's orders.

"Who's at the door, Zapata!" Cortina said from upstairs.

"It's Cerra and the boy," Zapata said.

"Well see what they want. I thought I made it clear I didn't want any interruptions."

"What do you want?" he said through the small opening in the door.

"I bring coffee and biscuits for El Jefe," Cerra said.

"They've brought coffee and biscuits for you, senor," Zapata said.

"Let them in," he said, "Some refreshments would be nice."

As he opened the door, the sound of gunshots echoed from the bunk house. Zapata brought his gun up and tried to shut the door, but the boy stepped forward to try and stop him.

"Who are you?" Zapata said. "You're not the kitchen boy."

"No, I'm not. My name's Tommy and I know you. You're the man who shot and stabbed my family. You butchered my little sister. She was only ten years old and you hacked her to death with your knife, but now God has delivered you into my hands."

Zapata cocked his pistol and stuck it out in front of him. As he prepared to fire, he was oblivious to the danger that stood directly beside him, nor did he likely hear the shot that entered the side of his head.

Jim looked down at the body of the outlaw, and said, "Thank you Cerra. Now please take Tommy back to the kitchen, while I finish my business here."

"Let me go with you," Tommy said, "I've still got the gun that Bob gave me."

"No, Tommy," he said. "You've had the satisfaction of seeing the one that killed your family get what was coming to him, but I must face Cortina by myself."

Stepping over the dead outlaw's body, Jim walked through the door to find Cortina.

Jim had hoped that Cortina would come out and either surrender, or fight him in the open. He was more than a match for most men in a straight up gun fight, but Cortina, like most outlaws, would seek every advantage he could get. Neither man had survived for so long in such dangerous professions by taking chances or by letting their opponents have the upper hand.

Cortina had chosen a position at the top of the landing, which commanded a view of the living room downstairs. From there he would be able to see anything that moved down below. For his part, Jim knew that if he could draw his fire, he might be able to get him to waste much of his ammo.

The Ranger never cared much for running, but now he ran as fast as he could for the winding staircase. He managed to stay one step ahead of Cortina's bullets as they struck the floor right behind him. As soon as he hit the bottom of the staircase, he continued up, firing with each step.

With nowhere else to run, Cortina made his stand, determined to either meet his fate or send the Ranger to his. At the top of the stairs the two faced off, and fired, but the hammers of both men's guns clicked on empty chambers. For just a moment, the enemies stared, unflinching, each waiting for the other to make the first move.

"Senor Cortina, I'm here to take you back to Texas to be tried for murder. Surrender now and we can avoid any further bloodshed," Jim said.

Cortina smiled a sly, slightly evil smile. "What do I have to go back to in Tejas, amigo?"

"Your trial and hanging, I suspect," Jim said.

"If it's all the same to you, I think no. I will pass on your kind invitation senor." Cortina raised his left hand, which held the coach gun he kept hidden as a last resort, but for the first time in his life he wasn't fast enough.

By the time Cortina looked his foe in the eye and resolved to fire, Jim had already squeezed the trigger of the pistol he had concealed behind his back. Cortina's body hit the floor with a loud thud, and with that, the Ranger's long odyssey was over.

The night breeze felt refreshing and brought Jim a much needed sense of calm as he stepped out into the moonlight. A wave of exhaustion had quickly replaced the adrenaline-fueled exuberance of only a few moments ago.

"I guess you got your man," a voice called from the shadows.

Jim looked up and saw the silhouette of his friend and protégé approaching. "Yeah, I got him alright," Jim said, "How about you? Did ya take any prisoners?"

"I got one still alive," Heck said.

"Well that's something, I reckon," Jim said. "Let's go check on Tommy. The kid did okay tonight. We may make a Ranger out of him yet."

"Maybe so," Heck said. "Ya know, the Captain's gonna be awfully upset we didn't take more prisoners. You know how he likes to have a good hangin' to show the people that law and order is being upheld."

"Well I guess this time the Captain and the good people of Texas will have to be satisfied with our word that justice was carried out," Jim said.

The two men walked into the kitchen, where Cerra was in the process of fixing some grub for the hungry Rangers.

"I make you some food. You look hungry," the cook said.

"That sounds good Cooky," Jim said. "We have quite a few graves to dig, and then we could use a day or two to rest ourselves and our horses. It's a long ride back to Texas and I'd like some sleep and a few hot meals before we head out. Now do you have any whiskey around this place? I think we could all use a drink."

CHAPTER THIRTY-TWO

It took the men several days to rest up and then get the cannon and crates of guns loaded up and ready to travel. It was slow going with the heavy wooden wagons and caissons, but luckily Cerra was looking for another opportunity, and agreed to help the Rangers bring their load back to Texas. It took some ingenuity on the part of the group to haul their heavy burden across the Rio Grande, but with a little thought and a lot of patience, they finally made it back to Texas.

Jim had decided the group should stay at Fort Brown for a day or two before heading on to San Antonio. As the four approached the fort, they were shocked to see that someone else had already taken up residence in the abandoned garrison. On the top of the rampart, the Lone Star Flag was flying high, gently fluttering in the wind.

As they entered the gates, they could see a couple of dozen men milling about, but they were all so preoccupied with their own tasks that they paid no mind to the three Rangers or the deadly cargo that they were transporting.

"Well, I'll be darned to Hades! I had about given up hope you'd make it back," a booming voice called from across the compound.

"Captain Hale," Jim said, "what are you doing here?"

"I'm commanding the new Ranger company and the Governor decided since this fort was not being used at the moment, it might make a good headquarters for the new company," the Captain said.

Heck looked around and said, "So, it's really happening? Texas is joining the Rebs?"

"Yes, son," he said, "I'm afraid so. We are officially at war and most men of fighting age have gone north. I have managed to keep ahold of a few to fill the company roster, but most of them are old men. They're mostly former soldiers and a few retired Rangers. Please come into my office. We can have some coffee and you can tell me everything that has happened."

The Captain's office was considerably larger than the one he occupied in San Antonio, but without the charm. In typical army fashion, the room was void of any decoration or other trappings of civility. The windowless room had more of a dungeon feel than that of an office. The building had been built with defense in mind instead of comfort, and there was not much fresh air that made it into the cavernous structure. What air there was, was stale and smelled of old wood and sweat.

The men entered the office and were each given a steaming cup of dark brown mud. "Where's Bob?" the Captain said. "Don't tell me you fellas made a drunk out of him and he's sitting over in the Brownsville saloon?"

"Bob's dead, Captain," Jim said. "He was killed a little over a week ago in the attack on Cortina's ranch."

"My God!" he said. "That is indeed a very sad piece of news, and also an immeasurable loss for the Rangers."

"Yes sir, that it is," Heck said. "We were able to accomplish our mission. Cortina and his militia are all dead, and as you can see we have retrieved the arms."

"I had no doubt you would. From the moment Private Mathias told me about the massacre and the stolen weapons, I knew you would stop at nothing to bring those outlaws to justice. I'm just sorry you couldn't bring me any prisoners."

"Well, captain, we had one prisoner, but what with having to transport the cannon and all, we decided to turn him into the local law in Hidalgo. He was wanted for crimes there and the good citizens seemed only too happy to take him off our hands. I doubt they will even wait for the gallows to be built," Jim said.

"That's of little loss to the cause of jurisprudence, I'm sure," the Captain said. "I am sorry about the death of Corporal Curtis, but I am very proud of all of you. You are indeed a credit to the State of Texas."

"Thank you, sir, but it must be said that young Tommy here acquitted himself in superb fashion, and was of considerable service," Heck said.

"Well, that's good to know. Perhaps it's time to make him an official sworn in Ranger," he said.

"He will make a fine Ranger," Heck said, "and he will make a good replacement for me."

"What do you mean a replacement for you?" Captain Hale said.

"Yeah, what are you talking about, kid?" Jim said.

"I mean, I have decided to join Captain McCullough and the Rebs."

"Mr. Carson, I must ask you to reconsider. You are a lawman not a soldier, and trust me you don't want to join this fight. Remember what I told you son, it's a hopeless cause," the Captain said.

"I know, you're probably right sir, but I just can't stay with the Rangers. I still want to fight for Texas, and the best way for me to do that, I reckon, is with the army. I just feel I must move on and find my place somewhere else."

"C'mon, Heck. This isn't our fight, and we don't owe the Rebels nothin'. They're a bunch of rich slavers and not worth one of our lives," Jim said.

"I've made up my mind. This is just something that I need to do."

"Well Mr. Carson, your loss will be felt, but a man must follow his conscience, no matter where it leads him," Captain Hale said. "The Third Texas Cavalry is still in San Antonio and gathering arms at the Alamo. I'm sure they will be glad to have you. I will spare Jim, Tommy and two others to help you deliver your guns."

"Thank you, sir," Heck said. "I appreciate your help and understanding."

"It's the least I can do for one of the best Rangers it's been my privilege to command."

ABOUT THE AUTHOR

JOHN SPIARS is a western writer and amateur historian with a passion for telling the stories of the American West. He lives in North Texas with his wife and four children. When not writing novels, he maintains a blog dedicated to Texas history and travel.

CONNECT ONLINE

underthelonestar.com

OTHER BOOKS BY JOHN SPIARS

Hell and Half of Texas: Heck Carson Series Volume 2

Bury me at Palmetto Creek

Made in the USA
Middletown, DE
25 November 2018